GOLD LUST

"Hold it, Captain," said Hawk, "don't come any closer."

The captain halted.

"What do you cutthroats want?"

"Hell, you mean you don't know?" asked the captain.

"Gold," answered Hawk.

"That's what I like," said the captain, "a man who says what's on his mind. Just hand it over and there'll be an end to this business."

"I don't have it."

"You expect me to believe that?"

"I don't care what you believe," said Hawk. He heard a movement behind him and a knife grazed his throat as a man threw him to the ground. Hawk relaxed, offering no resistance; he had been waiting for this moment. He flung his thighs upward, dislodging the attacker.

What he didn't see was the knife coming swiftly toward his throat. . . .

SIGNET (0451)

DOUBLE BARRELED ACTION!

☐ **GOLDEN HAWK by Will C. Knott.** His parents named him Jed Thompson, but when the Comanches killed them they adopted him and named him Golden Hawk. Equipped with fighting skills taught by Indian Warriors, and loving skills taught by passionate Indian women, he blazed a trail of vengeance, passion and adventures through the West at its wildest. . . . (144937—$2.50)

☐ **GOLDEN HAWK #2 BLOOD HUNT by Will C. Knott.** Hawk is on a rescue ride into redskin territory raging with raw sex and dealy violence. Golden Hawk's one-man war flamed with fury when he learned his beautiful sister was still a captive of a brutal Blackfoot chief. (145720—$2.50)

☐ **GOLDEN HAWK #3 GRIZZLY PASS by Will C. Knott.** A rock-hard hero—matching himself against the most bloodthirsty warriors and man-hungry women in the West. Golden Hawk is faced with cruel choices. He had never met an enemy he could not oufight or a woman he could not satisfy—but now he had to decide on which foe and which female he should take on. . . . (147502—$2.50)

☐ **GOLDEN HAWK #4: HELL'S CHILDREN.** Sex and savagery thrust Hawk into action against redskin violence and Blackfoot magic as Hawk must kill or be killed in his effort to guide a beautiful woman's wagon train through hostile redskin land. (148916—$2.50)

☐ **GOLDEN HAWK #5: KILL HAWK.** Hawk stands tall when savage killers lust for gold and luscious ladies lust for him. But even his best friends couldn't be trusted not to join the pack that wanted to grease their rush for gold with Hawk's blood. . . . (149661—$2.50)

Buy them at your local bookstore or use this convenient coupon for ordering.

NEW AMERICAN LIBRABY,
P.O. Box 999, Bergenfield, New Jersey 07621

Please send me the books I have checked above. I am enclosing $_________.
(please add $1.00 to this order to cover postage and handling). Send check or money order—no cash or C.O.D.'s. Prices and numbers subject to change without notice.

Name ____________________________________

Address __________________________________

City ____________ State __________ Zip Code ________

Allow 4-6 weeks for delivery.
This offer is subject to withdrawal without notice.

GOLDEN HAWK 5

KILL HAWK

Will C. Knott

A SIGNET BOOK
NEW AMERICAN LIBRARY

PUBLISHER'S NOTE

This book is a work of fiction. Names, characters, places, and incidents either are the product of the author's imagination or are used fictitiously, and any resemblance to actual persons, living or dead, events, or locales is entirely coincidental.

NAL BOOKS ARE AVAILABLE AT QUANTITY DISCOUNTS WHEN USED TO PROMOTE PRODUCTS OR SERVICES. FOR INFORMATION PLEASE WRITE TO PREMIUM MARKETING DIVISION, NEW AMERICAN LIBRARY, 1633 BROADWAY, NEW YORK, NEW YORK 10019.

Copyright © 1987 by Will C. Knott

All rights reserved

SIGNET TRADEMARK REG. U.S. PAT. OFF. AND FOREIGN COUNTRIES
REGISTERED TRADEMARK—MARCA REGISTRADA
HECHO EN CHICAGO, U.S.A.

SIGNET, SIGNET CLASSIC, MENTOR, ONYX, PLUME, MERIDIAN and NAL BOOKS are published by NAL PENGUIN INC., 1633 Broadway, New York, New York 10019

First Printing, September, 1987

1 2 3 4 5 6 7 8 9

PRINTED IN THE UNITED STATES OF AMERICA

GOLDEN HAWK

A quiet stream under the Comanche moon . . . leaping savages . . . knives flashing in the firelight . . . brutal, shameful death . . .

Ripped from the bosom of their slain parents and carried off by the raiding Comanches, Jed Thompson and his sister can never forget that hellish night under the glare of the Comanche moon, seared into their memories forever.

Years later, his vengeance slaked, pursued relentlessly by his past Comanche brothers, Jed is now Golden Hawk. Half Comanche, half white man. A legend in his time, an awesome nemesis to some—a bulwark and a refuge to any man or woman lost in the terror of that raw, savage land.

— Prologue —

Hawk stirred suddenly and sat up on his cot. Something outside the cabin had awakened him. He reached for the Hawken he kept primed and ready beside his cot. Then he sat quietly, not moving a muscle, barely breathing, as he listened.

But he heard nothing—only the birds coming awake with the dawn, their bright chatter echoing in the timber. Hawk frowned, perplexed. He could not shake his certainty that something outside the cabin had awakened him. For a few moments longer he waited without moving, every sense alert.

Then he reached back into his thick, shoulder-length thatch of blond hair to make sure his throwing knife rested in its leather sheath at the nape of his neck. Still holding the rifle, he got to his feet. He was a big, powerfully built man over six feet tall with a sun-bronzed, rawboned face and a sharp beak of a nose. As he crossed to the window, his naked frame loomed ominously in the cabin's dim interior. He peered across the misty clearing at the stand of timber beyond, resembling as he did so an intent bird of prey.

His keen blue eyes saw nothing out of the ordinary, and he moved over to the door and pressed his ear against it. This time he heard something. Pulling open the door, he stepped outside. He had not been hearing things. Not twenty feet from the corner of his cabin, a horse was standing in the yard, with what looked like an unconscious rider sprawled across its back.

Moving hurriedly toward the horse, Hawk saw that its rider had somehow managed to tie himself to it. He had been shot. Under his shoulder blade, an entry wound was clearly visible. The rider's face was turned away from him. He was hatless and his buckskin shirt and pants hung in tatters from his frame. Ripped and slashed by repeated brushings against rocks and bushes, the man's exposed skin appeared as raw as fresh beefsteak. When he got closer, Hawk realized the man had sustained a head wound as well. The horse's flanks trembled continuously. Blood from the wounded rider covered its neck clear down to its shoulders, and the mane itself was dark with clots.

The rider had wound rawhide about his waist, passed it under the horse's belly, then managed to wrap it around the saddle horn. Hawk cut the rider free, flung him over his shoulder, and carried him into his cabin. Letting him down as gently as possible onto his cot, Hawk thought he recognized the wounded man, but couldn't be sure—not with his face in this shape.

The right half had been laid open from brow to chin. From the look of it, a blow from a rifle barrel had done most of the damage, crushing the cheekbone so severely that the right eye was gone from its socket. Encrusted blood caked the man's shattered nostrils and torn, swollen lips, and his jawline was grotesquely out of line, indicating that the jaw was broken as well, the damage stemming from that single terrible blow.

The man was still breathing. His encrusted lips moved just barely and the man's single eye flickered open. Hawk leaned close, sure now he knew this man.

"Got here, didn't I, Hawk?" he whispered softly.

The voice did it. This was Pete Foxwell, a free trapper who worked the mountains around Taos. It was said he had found and trapped streams that not even the Utes could locate. On a trip to Taos two years ago with Old Bill Williams, Hawk and Old Bill had swapped stories with him for a long, convivial night.

"What the hell happened to you, Pete?"

"Ran into some varmints—the two legged variety." Pete coughed up red spittle. "There's a bullet in my back, Hawk."

"I saw. Lay still and I'll take it out."

Hawk left Pete to build up the fire, then began to hone his throwing knife. It had a blade longer and narrower than his bowie, which made it better for probing. As he sharpened the blade, Pete watched him from the cot, his breathing labored. He was obviously in considerable pain.

"How long you been on that horse?" Hawk asked.

"A day and a night."

"What in hell happened, Pete?"

"That new trader in Taos . . . has been cheatin'

me, Hawk, and all the other trappers. So I got even. Walked in, threw him a pile of plews, and took his gold in payment . . . before he could send it to California for safekeeping."

"That wasn't smart, Pete."

"Know it. Anyway, the son of a bitch sent a small army of bounty-hunters after me. Turned out . . . they weren't interested in gettin' his gold back to him."

"They got the gold back, didn't they?"

"Nope. I hid most of it before they caught up with me."

"Is that why they worked you over? So you'd tell them where you hid it?"

Pete nodded, closed his eyes, and coughed a couple of times weakly. After a few moments, he opened his remaining eye.

"And when they asked you where you hid it, you turned stubborn."

Pete nodded. At once he began to cough weakly—— it was clear any movement at all caused him great distress. He opened his eye and spoke in a low, harsh whisper. "Why should I tell them where I hid it? The gold's mine. I'm the one who took it."

"You old bastard."

What passed for a grin broke the planes of Pete's terribly ravaged face, then his body twisted in a sudden spasm of pain.

Hawk walked over to him and laid his hand on Pete's shoulder. "Lay still, Pete," Hawk told him, leaning close. "Don't say any more until I cut out that bullet."

Hawk went back to the fireplace. The flames were leaping high by this time. He passed the blade repeatedly through them until it was glowing, then returned to the cot. Rolling Pete gently over onto his stomach, he began his probe for the bullet, doing his best to get in and out fast.

The stench of singed flesh was strong in his nostrils by the time he worked the ball out of Pete's back. As Hawk's probing blade worked deep, the trapper had not cried out once or uttered a single moan, and when Hawk turned him gently over onto his back, he found out why.

Pete Foxwell was dead.

Not until after Hawk had buried Pete Foxwell under a rude stone cairn above his cabin did he find out what the trapper meant when he told Hawk he had hidden "most" of the gold.

Inside of Pete's saddlebag, Hawk found a small leather pouch filled with gold coins. Emptying the gold onto his kitchen table, he sat down and began to count. Sitting back in his chair a moment later, he contemplated the neat stacks of gold coins. He had close to three hundred dollars. A small fortune.

Hawk let his imagination soar. He would purchase some new traps and then the tools he needed for the cabin—a new hammer, a wheelbarrow, shovels, and a pickax. He would stockpile gunpowder, firing caps, and lead for casting bullets. He needed a new blade for his hatchet as well. For weeks now he had been thinking about building a shed in back for his horses. With nails it would be much quicker and easier to construct.

He got up from his table and stretched. He was sorry Pete was gone. The presence of death hung in the air, but he would shake that soon enough, he reckoned, when he set out for Fort Hall.

—1—

The beer stein missed Hawk's head and shattered against the wall. Hawk jumped up. Two men were locked in a drunken brawl on the far side of the room. The fracas ended abruptly when a fellow wielding what looked like a steel truncheon caught one of them smartly on the head. The brawler slumped forward over the table, out cold. The fellow with the truncheon hurried over to Hawk and Dick Wootton's table.

"Allow me to introduce myself," he said. "Captain John Smollett, at your service. Sorry about that glass. Nearly hit you, didn't it?"

"It came too damn close for comfort," Hawk told him.

"Now, you mustn't mind these here shipmates of mine. This marlinspike will keep them quiet. Don't you fret."

"Is that what you used?" Dick asked, glancing at the heavy iron club still in the captain's grasp.

"Yes, guv'nor," the captain said, lifting the

weapon, "and a hard master it is—as many of me crew can testify."

Captain Smollett was a tall, rangy fellow with sharp, knifelike features. From under his white, visored captain's cap, a straw-colored cowlick flopped down over his forehead.

Hawk took up his mug of rum. "Just remind that crewman of yours, Captain, that if there's any more foolishness, I'll send him headfirst through that wall over there."

"I'll be sure to tell him that, guv'nor. Yessir, and thank you for being so patient with the likes of us poor sailors lost in this land without the comfort of a heaving deck under our feet."

Curious, Hawk stared at the captain. There was something about the man that didn't ring true. Though he introduced himself as a ship's captain, Hawk doubted that Smollett had ever commanded anything larger than a rowboat.

"Captain did you say?" Hawk said.

Smollett nodded firmly. "I see you question that, guv'nor, and I don't blame you. There's no smell of the sea about me. But it's the truth, more's the pity lost adrift as we are in this savage wild. But I was a captain."

"Where's your ship?"

"At the bottom of the sea."

"Too bad."

"Yes, guv'nor, it was," Smollett replied.

With a casual salute, the captain returned to his charges. They were once again making a stir, but with a few cuffs and a sharp word or two, the captain quieted them down. A surly, grumbling silence came over the men.

The settlers and a few teamsters sitting around the room seemed relieved that the sailors were being kept quiet by the captain. Linus MacDuff, the Hudson's Bay functionary who kept open this small grog shop in back of his commissary, hurried over to Hawk's table. He was a small, wiry redhead with rust-colored eyebrows that beetled out over his light-green eyes.

"I'm telling you, gents," he said, mopping his brow as he bent over their table. "Those fellows are a mean bunch. I don't mind telling you that I don't like the look of them."

"Where'd they come from?" asked Dick Wootton.

"They just trailed in here, one by one, more than a week ago."

"A strange lot," Dick commented, glancing over at them.

There appeared to be at least a dozen or more, occupying half of the grog shop, their chairs all pulled up around one large table. They were not quiet. They argued volubly, incessantly, their voices shrill, their conversation sprinkled with salty oaths that only men of the sea favored.

"What'll you have, gents?" Linus asked.

"More rum," Hawk told him.

Linus left with their empty jug.

Leaning back in his chair, Dick glanced at Captain Smollett. "A captain, is he? What do you think, Hawk?"

"He's a fraud, pure and simple. More than likely he's an ordinary seaman who jumped ship with his buddies. He probably stole that officer's cap."

With a quick nod of agreement, Dick swung his attention back to Hawk. "You still planning to leave in the morning?"

"No reason not to."

"Looks like you're turning that cabin of yours into a farm. All them nails. Are you sure you aren't thinking of building a henhouse?"

"I just want more room and a shed for the horses."

That morning Dick Wootton had ridden into Fort Hall to find Hawk in the act of purchasing two pack horses from a shifty-eyed Arikawa. Both men had been well-pleased to come upon each other once again, and for the remainder of the day Wootton helped Hawk shop for goods. Though it must have been a surprising sight to see Hawk pay for what he had purchased in gold coin, up until now the trapper had not asked how Hawk had come upon his sudden wealth. But he must have wondered. And Hawk knew he was bursting to know.

Linus brought the new jug of rum. As Dick filled his and Hawk's glass, he glanced over at Hawk, a glint in his eyes. "What'd you do, Hawk? Rob a bank?"

Hawk pulled his rum closer. "You remember a trapper named Pete Foxwell?"

Dick thought for a minute, then nodded. "Yeah, I remember. He's the one still trapping around Taos, isn't he?"

"That's the one."

"He gave you that money?"

"He didn't give it to me. I took it from his saddlebag after he died."

Dick Wootton leaned suddenly closer. "What happened?"

"Seems the poor son of a bitch lost his patience with that new trader in Taos and stole his gold. A posse took after him. But it wasn't much interested in bringing back the trader's gold. They wanted it for themselves."

"Did they get it?"

Hawk shook his head. "Before they caught up to Foxwell, he buried it somewhere."

"You know where?"

"No, and this here gold I found in his saddlebag is all I want."

"You've sure been spending it fast."

"Easy come, easy go."

"Reckon you're right, at that."

"Maybe I should've sent this gold back to that trader in Taos. But I didn't much like what I've been hearing about him."

"Forget him, Hawk. You won't be hearing any more about him."

"Why not?"

"He's dead, too. A few Indians he cheated came after him. They took his scalp and his balls—I don't know in what order." Dick grinned. "Keep the gold. The bastard won't be needing it."

Hawk should have felt relieved, but he didn't. He still felt uneasy whenever he felt the weight of the heavy pouch dangling from his belt. As soon as he had begun purchasing goods that day, a kind of fever had swept over him. He had seemed determined, almost eager, to rid himself of the gold.

An irate series of cries erupted from Captain Smollett's crew. Hawk glanced over. Smollett was trying to keep his men quiet, but his was only one shrill voice among many. The angry cries rose to a crescendo, sounding like a full harness of sled dogs caught in a fire. The settlers and teamsters hurried from the place, but Hawk was not about to be chased and did his best to ignore the commotion.

He turned back to Dick. "Why not stay at my cabin for a while? The hunting's good, and getting better. The elk are drifting back up into the higher valleys and there's plenty of mule deer."

"I'd like to, Hawk, and I thank you for the invitation, but I got my eye on a Flathead girl not far from here. She is really pretty and shy. I think a couple of good horses and a rifle might be all I need to buy her."

Suddenly a hurtling body struck Hawk with the impact of a cannonball. The blow slammed his head sharply against the wall. Hawk's chair, the table, and the jug of rum crashed with him to the floor, and he found himself alongside the fellow who had struck him. There was a butcher knife in his hand, a wild look in his eye—he stank of rum and vomit.

Before Hawk could grab him, the fellow sprang to his feet to meet the rush of the fellow who had flung him across the room. He had a knife out also. The two crashed clumsily into each other. Too drunk for any decisive blows, they proceeded to dance about each other, slashing and parrying, doing their drunken best to cut each other's throat. Smollett's crew joined in and a wild, confusing melee commenced.

As Hawk scrambled away from the wreckage, he saw Smollett trying to pull the combatants apart, but they were rum-sodden madmen by this time and turned with a fury on their keeper, driving him back. Like a fire out of control the free-for-all raged with rising intensity, the battlers using chairs, knives, and the butts of their pistols in a melee that threatened to destroy every stick of furniture in the grog shop.

Wringing his hands in an excess of alarm, Linus rushed over to help Hawk and Dick to their feet. "You must stop them," he cried. "Please! They'll wreck the place."

Hawk needed no excuse. He was furious. With Dick at his side, he waded into the wild crowd, selecting two men battering each other with rungs from a ruined chair. He finished the nearest one with a powerful rabbit punch and caught the second with a swift kick in the crotch. As the man doubled over, Hawk grabbed him by the ears, twisted him completely around, and ran his head into the wall. Crunching heavily into it, the fellow sagged to the floor.

A warning shout came from Dick. Hawk turned. One of the crew was coming at him with a long butcher knife. He held it extended like a bayonet. Hawk sidestepped. As he did so, his pouch of coins came loose and hurtled to the floor, the gold spilling out in a glittering stream. Startled, Hawk's attacker paused to glance down at it. Hawk stepped forward, grabbed his wrist, and twisted. The sailor dropped his knife and screamed. Still holding the man's wrist, Hawk swung the man around once, twice, and then slammed him against the wall. Peeling off it like a swatted fly, the man fell to the floor.

Dick had been punishing a few of the seamen as well. Between the two of them, they had caused considerable damage. Swaying uncertainly, the men stopped pounding one another and glared around at Hawk and Dick.

"Hold it, gents," Smollett cried, hurrying over to Hawk. "There's no call for you to get mixed up in this."

Dick was in the act of punishing one miscreant. He had twisted the fellow's arm up behind his back and was still holding it. Sweat was streaming down the sailor's face as he stood on tiptoes to escape the terrible, excruciating pressure that threatened to snap off his arm.

Staring angrily at the captain, Dick increased the upward pressure on the sailor's arm. "Call off your crew, Captain. They're wrecking the place. If you can't stop them, Hawk and I will."

Smollett swung about to face his crewmen. "Get back to the table," he told them, his voice cold with anger. "Go on now! Or I'll break open your fool, empty skulls with me iron pet here."

As he spoke he shook his marlinspike at them. The men avoided the fury in Smollett's eyes and started back to their table. Seeing this, Dick flung the sailor he had been holding after them. The crew was now a sorry mess. Added to the damage Hawk and Dick Wootton had visited upon them was the woeful destruction they inflicted on themselves.

"Get out of here," cried Linus, running up. "All of you!"

He was standing next to Hawk and Dick Wootton as he spoke, and Smollett decided not to argue. "You heard him, you damned lubbers," the captain told his crew. "I've got no pity for you. Get out of here and return to your quarters!"

One of them pushed himself closer to Smollett. "You can't tell us what to do, Captain! We ain't at sea no more."

"Is that a fact, Olly?"

"It is, and you know it yourself, Captain. We's on dry land now."

With the speed of a striking rattler, Smollett came around with his marlinspike. The blow caught the upstart on the side of his head and sent him hurtling backward. He reduced a chair to kindling and came to rest in its wreckage, unconscious.

"Any more of you blokes want to question my authority?" the captain demanded. He seemed eager to use his marlinspike again.

No one else felt up to confronting the captain.

"All right then, mateys," Smollett told the men, his tone a bit more conciliatory. "You've had enough for one evening. Go on back to your quarters."

As Smollett's crew ambled toward the door, carrying their casualties with them, Hawk noticed that one of them was blind, feeling along the wall as he went. His face was lifted slightly and he wore that concentrated, intent look so many blind men have. Hawk recalled seeing the sailor in the thick of the melee, dishing out terrible blows to all who came within reach of his hickory stick. Refusing any help from those around him, he strode out into the night as boldly as anyone with two good eyes, his hickory stick jabbing the air ahead of him.

Once they were gone, Hawk gathered up his gold coins and once more fastened the heavy leather pouch to his belt. Captain Smollett had remained behind. Now he looked hopefully at Hawk and Dick Wootton, obviously hoping they would invite him to their table. But both men ignored Smollett and sat back down at one of the few undamaged tables.

"He wants us to invite him over," said Dick, glancing sidelong at the captain.

"Ignore him."

Linus hurried over to thank them profusely for

their aid in quelling the disturbance, after which he insisted that any more drinks would be on the house.

"In that case," replied Dick Wootton, "bring us out whiskey in a bottle, Linus—no more of that rotgut."

"Of course, of course! You shall have the best," Linus promised them warmly, hurrying off.

Unable to keep himself away, Captain Smollett approached their table, his tall figure bent slightly, his hands clasped humbly before him. There was no help for it, Hawk realized.

"Why don't you sit down and join us, Captain?" Hawk suggested. "Otherwise, you'll trip over our table."

"Why, don't mind if I do, gents," Captain Smollett said, pulling up a chair. "I sure hope you two wasn't injured in that unfortunate tangle."

"We'll survive," allowed Dick Wootton.

Linus arrived with the freshly opened whiskey bottle. He had seen the captain at their table and brought three glasses. Hawk filled the captain's glass. Raising his glass in a quick salute, Smollett threw the whiskey down his throat as casually as he would a glass of water.

"Much obliged, gents," he said, wiping his mouth with the back of his hand. "There ain't nothin' better than whiskey from a bottle." He refilled his glass.

"Don't hold back none," Dick said.

"Why, thank you, matey," Smollett replied, downing only half of his drink this time. "Tell me, friend," he said, addressing Hawk, "weren't those genuine gold coins I saw spilling out of that pouch of yours?"

"That's an impertinent question, mister."

Smollett help up his hand. "Now, guv'nor, I was just curious, is all. There seemed to be such a heap of them." He smiled. "Nothin's as pretty as gold coins in lamplight, or as pleasant and comforting as the sound they make chinking in a full buckskin pouch."

"Why does that gold make you curious?" Dick asked.

"Isn't that obvious? How come a trapper this deep in the wilderness would come upon such riches? Why, them coins was all fresh-minted." He smiled at Hawk. "Looks like your friend here's found that pot of gold at the end of the rainbow. Either that or he done stole it."

Dick said, "Where I come from, Captain, talking like that can get a man in a heap of trouble."

"You're right, mate. Another man's gold ain't none of my business, and that's the pure and simple truth of it. It don't matter if he stole or found it."

"Nice of you," Hawk commented ironically.

Smollett reached for the bottle. About then Linus and the two others were doing what they could to clear away the wrecked tables and chairs and replace them with serviceable substitutes. The captain paid them no heed, ignoring completely the havoc his men had done to the place.

"I noticed one of your crew is blind, Captain," Hawk said.

Smollett refilled his glass. Then he took off his captain's cap and brushed the unruly cowlick that had worked down over his forehead. The cap needed cleaning. "So you noticed Old Tim Prew, did you?"

"He looked quite fearsome."

The captain nodded solemnly. "Struck blind, was Old Tim by the cruel hand of a drunken first mate. Afterward, he was kept on to serve as cabin boy, and used most cruelly, I assure you."

"And now he is under your wing, Captain?"

"That he is."

"You got a pretty damned unholy crew there," Dick reminded him coldly. "And you still ain't told us what you're doing in these parts."

"Why, just like them settlers who run out of here, we're looking for our fortunes, like any who brave this wild continent. Just like you, gents, trapping fur and leading settlers to new homes. This here's a land where mighty things can happen. Yessir, its a land where a man can kick dirt off his boots and find gold."

Both men looked at each other. Hawk had finally made up his mind about the captain. He was a fraud, all right. He was also a windbag. One prick with a pin and he'd blow clear to hell. Hawk's nod to Dick Wootton was barely perceptible. A second later the two men got to their feet.

"Good night, Captain," Hawk said.

"Why, gents," the captain cried, glancing in mild panic at the bottle of whiskey, "the night is young."

"Stay here, then, and finish the bottle," Hawk told him.

"With our compliments," said Dick.

"Why, that's most generous, lads. Thank you kindly," he responded, smiling broadly as he also got to his feet. "But I'm sure you won't mind if I just take it along with me and share its contents. Much obliged."

"I don't like him," Dick said a moment later as

the door closed behind the captain. "That old windbag is trouble."

"That's right," said Hawk. "He's dangerous. He's liable to bore you to death."

Laughing, both men followed the captain out.

Alone in his room, Hawk peeled off his buckskins and sat for a while on his bed. The rum was still buzzing in his head. A bright moon sat on the far horizon, sending a clean, almost intrusive light into the darkened room.

After a moment Hawk walked over to the window to peer out at the moonlit landscape and thought of his cabin. For the past six months he had been putting hard work into it, turning it more and more into a home. What he had bought this day would make it even more so, and by next year he hoped to have a roof completely shingled. Despite Dick's crack, however, he would never allow chickens to scratch about in his front yard. It would be his castle, not another settler's roost.

There was a cry at his door. Not sure he had heard right, Hawk spun about. The cry came again, muffled this time. It sounded like someone in pain. He crossed the room and flung the door open. Dick Wootton, still upright, fell into his arms. Hawk propelled him across the room to the bed. As Dick collapsed facedown onto it, Hawk saw the knife sticking out of his back.

Outside the doorway he heard running footsteps. Snatching up his revolver, Hawk raced from the room in time to see a running figure heading for the fort gate. Hawk followed. As he ran through the open gate, a knife flew at him, embedding itself in the palisade wall inches from his face.

Hawk stopped and waited.

The knife thrower ran out from behind one of the Indian tepees that stood close under the fort's wall. In a few swift strides, Hawk overtook him and swung him around. At once he found himself struggling with an insensate, snarling old man, whose intensity reminded Hawk of the mindless fury of a cornered wolverine. With a powerful punch to his face and a second to his gut Hawk drove the man into the ground, then slammed his foot into the small of his back and let him twist helplessly under it.

"Digger," the fellow yelled hoarsely. "Digger, where are you?"

Only then did Hawk realize he had been struggling with the blind man. He felt momentarily troubled—until he realized how close the fellow had just come to killing him.

Again the blind man cried out. "Digger!"

There was a slight, furtive rustling behind Hawk. Before he could turn, he heard the swish of a heavy weapon a second before it struck his skull.

All was a black void.

— 2 —

A Crow woman was bent over him, her magnificent dark eyes luminous with concern. The gray light of dawn lightened the tepee's walls. The woman was wearing nothing above her waist, her buckskin skirt little more than an apron to cover her thighs. He would have reached up to take her in his arms, but any movement caused a violent eruption inside his head.

The woman must have caught sight of him sprawled on the ground and carried him inside the lodge. Turning his head slightly, he saw another Crow woman watching him intently. An older Crow warrior was sitting cross-legged on the other side of the hearth, watching intently, a clay pipe in his mouth.

"I send to fort. Tell of you," the Crow woman told him in very poor English.

"I speak Crow," Hawk told her.

She just nodded and continued to apply cold compresses to his forehead. The concern she felt for him was apparent in her face. Hawk tried to smile up at her, but even that slight movement caused his brain to come unglued.

The sound of running feet could be heard approaching the tepee and a moment later Linus MacDuff and Dennis Clerman, the Hudson's Bay chief factor, burst into the lodge. With dignity the Crow warrior got to his feet and waited for the two men to offer some explanation for this breach of good manners.

But Linus and Clerman paid no heed to the Crow. Ignoring the Crow woman, Linus helped Hawk to his feet. For a moment the tepee interior spun around him. Hawk clung to Linus, then allowed himself to be helped from the Crow lodge. He wanted to hold up to thank the Crow woman, but Linus and Clerman allowed no time for that as they helped him quickly back into the fort.

"Dick Wootton's in my room," Hawk told Linus. "He's been stabbed and needs help."

"That's already been taken care of," Clerman assured him. "Right now he's resting up in my quarters. Your door was wide open and the whole damn fort heard him bawling for someone to take that dagger out of his back."

"How is he?"

"Doc Squires says he'll be all right. But it'll be a few weeks before he goes after that Flathead girl."

"How do you feel?" Linus asked him.

"Never mind that. What's this all about? Why did that blind man stab Dick?"

"A blind man?" Clerman asked.

"Yes, dammit."

"You sure of it?"

"Never mind that. What's going on here?"

"You were robbed last night, Hawk," Linus said ruefully. "That's what you get for flashing gold coins around here."

So that was it. Those men had been after his gold. He should have known.

"We wondered where the hell you'd gone to," Linus said, obviously relieved. "I thought maybe Smollett had carried you off along with the gold."

"Then he and that crew of his have lit out."

Clerman nodded. "Like the thieves they were," he said bitterly, "the entire miserable lot of them."

"I think I want to talk to Dick."

"You think you're up to it? You don't look so good."

"I'm up to it."

Clerman nodded. "He'll be glad to see you, too."

Sitting up in Clerman's bed, Dick Wootton's entire upper torso was swathed in bandages. He looked very uncomfortable, but at the sight of Hawk he brightened considerably.

"You don't look so good yourself," Dick commented as Hawk peered down at the mountain man.

"My head's pounding some," Hawk admitted. "Now, what in hell were you doing at my door last night with a knife in your back?"

"I was coming to warn you," Dick said ironically.

"You did a fine job."

"I suppose you know already, Hawk. You've been robbed."

"So I understand."

"I was on my way to my room when I overheard that crew planning to break into your room for the gold." He shrugged. "They got me before I could get to you."

"And I gave them a clear shot at the gold when I rushed out."

"It's a good thing you did. If you'd stayed behind, those bastards would've taken you down. They were drunk when they left the grog shop, but they were cold-sober planning this. That son of a bitch Smollett is a pirate. It was gunboats, not bad weather that sent his ship to the bottom."

There was a knock on the door. Hawk answered it and found a pretty, round-faced Flathead woman in the doorway. An old, white-haired Indian, obviously her father, stood behind her.

Hawk looked back at Dick. There was a pleased grin on his face.

Stepping back, Hawk allowed the Flathead girl and her father into the room. Then he left Dick alone with the girl and her father. Dick did not seem at all unhappy to see him go. He had a bargaining session coming up for the hand of a very beautiful Flathead maiden.

Hawk returned to his own quarters. His sleeping bag and the rest of his gear were still in the corner. The Hawken was leaning against the wall, his powder horn and bullet pouch dangling from the barrel, just as he had left them.

Good riddance then to the captain. The gold he took had not been Hawk's in the first place. Let the son of a bitch have it.

Hawk decided to go back to the Crow lodge and thank the Crows for taking care of him through the night. But the tepee was empty. Returning to the trading post, he found the two daughters and their father trading their plews and sable skins. The Crow woman was pleased to see him again. He asked what her name was, and she said Raven Eyes. It was appropriate. Her eyes were hauntingly beautiful, with a deep, somber quality that made it difficult for Hawk not to stare. Her sister was called Morning Star and Black Horse was her father.

Hawk stayed close as the Crows traded for blankets and other goods, keeping a sharp eye on each transaction to make sure they weren't cheated. The chief trader's assistant was not all pleased at Hawk's watchful presence, but the Crows understood the reason for it and were grateful. The trading completed, Hawk went back with them to their tepee and smoked awhile with Black Horse until exhaustion overtook him with a startling urgency and he returned to his own quarters.

Once there, he fell at once into a deep, dreamless sleep.

A soft rap on his door awakened him. It was close to dusk. He blinked the sleep from his eyes, aware that the pounding in his head was almost completely gone. He swung his feet off the bed and scratched his head. The rap came again.

"Who is it?"

"Raven Eyes."

He got up quickly and opened the door. Raven Eyes slipped into his room. He closed the door and in some surprise turned to look upon her, thinking of this morning when he had regained consciousness to find her bending over him, her breasts bared, her dark nipples erect. It seemed she was thinking the same thing.

"My father say I can stay with you this night."

Hawk smiled. "That's right decent of him."

Taking a couple of steps back, she lifted her buckskin dress, pulled it over her head, and flung it aside.

His eyes feasted on her slim, dusky body, especially her breasts. Not all that large, they were firmly round, provocative mounds with dark nipples and darker circles around each. His eyes feasted on the rest of her, drinking in the fresh nakedness of her fully rounded hips, outthrust belly, and below it, her gleaming black triangle.

He stepped swiftly out of his buckskin trousers, threw his shirt onto the small pile her dress made, then moved quickly forward, enclosing her waist with one hand and pressing her hard against him, his throbbing shaft probing for her triangle.

Eagerly, she led him over to the bed and pulled him down beside her, her legs closing around him at once, her rounded belly lifting. Her arms circled his neck and pulled his head forward onto her breasts. As he pulled on one and then the other nipple, she let out tiny delighted cries. He wasn't inside her yet, and she was lifting and pumping, pushing up for him, and he felt the wetness of her against him.

"Now! Now!" she told him fiercely, almost angrily.

He felt her mouth against his chest, biting, and pushed her back. Her round face came against him again, her hands suddenly caressing, and she moaned as her legs moved up and down the back of his thighs. His erection found the dark wetness of her and entered swiftly, pushing deep. She thrust upward against him in a continuous series of violent thrustings until she cried out. He halted, held back a moment, then rammed still deeper, and she exploded with wild pumping motions, which he answered with repeated slamming thrusts.

She grunted after each thrust, matching his frenzy with her own wild fervency. The first warning he had that she was coming was the sudden quivering of her belly. Letting out a wild, keening cry, she flung her head back and came in a series of tiny explosions, her thighs closing into his sides like soft vises, her climax ending in a gasp that seemed to pull every ounce of energy out of her. He kept on intently, touching bottom with each thrust. When he came, she clung to him so she could feel his powerful contractions deep inside her. Then she collapsed beneath him.

Panting, he slid off her, aware suddenly of how drained he felt. For a moment he let his eyes caress her as he took in her magnificent, savage loveliness. For a moment they both dozed off. When he opened his eyes, he reached out gently and took one of her breasts in his big hand and cupped it. She sighed and leaned closer to kiss him a long, open-mouth kiss.

"You are big again," she whispered, her hand reaching down into his crotch to fondle him.

He continued to suck on each breast. Her tiny cries became harsh groans and her body began pumping blindly toward him and he could sense her desire for more harsh, wild lovemaking. He grabbed her buttocks and swept her closer, then plunged deep into her. She climaxed once, twice, her deep, satisfied grunts urging him on to greater thrusts until he too came, clinging to her tightly as he expended his seed deep into her.

Collapsing beside her, he became aware of his labored breathing. She turned to him finally, her dark, fathomless eyes gazing fondly on him. Her face still flushed, tiny beads of perspiration covering her bronzed nakedness, she moved closer to him and kissed him boldly, passionately. . . .

They spent the night satisfying each other's needs until, spent utterly, they slept like stones in each other's arms. A slanting ray of sunlight pouring in through the window roused them soon after dawn. Coming awake slowly, Raven Eyes stretched, then reached out and pulled Hawk closer, then swung her hips over him. She rubbed her dense bush back and forth against his flaccid penis. His drowsiness vanished as he felt himself beginning to respond.

As soon as he was up, she uttered a deep, husky laugh and plunged down onto his erection. Leaning back, he let her have her way with him. She pressed down, writhing, twisting atop him, taking all of him into her, then plunged down again and again. He felt the slick sweetness of her pounding against his pelvic bones as she built to her release. Afterward, her head resting forward onto his powerful chest, hardly aware of his own building tension until this moment, Hawk came with a sudden, scalding rush and shot all he had up into her.

She rolled off him limply, legs still half atop him, and for a long delicious while they remained in each other's embrace as the sun slowly crept across the windowsill.

"Not a bad way to start the day," Hawk said finally.

She murmured her agreement.

"How much longer are you going to be at this fort?"

"My sister Morning Star and my father are eager to leave for our village this morning."

"Too bad."

"My father has already accepted the gifts of a trapper near our village. I will be his woman and live with him in his cabin."

"I'm happy for you."

"He is old, this one. When I find you on the ground, I see how hard your body is. You have fine broad shoulders. They are not like this trapper. One last time I must enjoy the body of a real man." She traced a circle around one of his nipples with her forefinger, then leaned forward and blew on his erect nipple. "What will you do now?"

"I have a cabin in the mountains. Soon as I can, I'm going back up there. I'll be glad to rid myself of this place. I don't like having so many people around me."

"You will not chase those men who took your gold?"

"I don't want the gold."

"This is very strange."

"Not for me, Raven Eyes."

She shrugged her indifference, but he was not sure she hadn't lost a little respect for him. To a Crow a man is not allowed to accept lightly the wrongs done him by another.

"Are you disappointed I won't be going after them?"

For an answer, she pulled him close and kissed him, her mouth yawning open, inviting his tongue.

He answered her kiss and with a short laugh rolled onto her and thrust her thighs aside. She reached down and guided him into her, uttering a sigh that was more like a purr.

"My father waits for me," she whispered as he straddled her and began thrusting slowly, easily. "We must leave the fort soon."

Hawk paid no attention. Black Horse would just have to wait a little longer for his daughter.

— 3 —

Opening the door to his cabin, Hawk peered out. The moon cast a pale sheen over the field. What had awakened him was a pitiable whine—almost human in its plaintiveness. Lifting his rifle, he left the cabin and circled it.

A wolf was crouching in the grass.

It was a big, handsome male with a light, silvery coat and a pure white ruff. Its ears sat up alertly, its eyes glowing with intelligence—and something else. Pain, perhaps? Or hope.

Hawk approached warily. As soon as he was within a few feet of the wolf, he saw how cruelly its belly had been torn up. The lacerations had scabbed over some, but they looked recent, and one wound was already festering. From the depth and extent of the wounds, Hawk surmised that the wolf had tangled with a wolverine. Once, from a safe distance, Hawk had watched a wolverine take a grizzly's kill from it after laying the bear open with similar wounds.

Hawk understood the wolf's dilemma. So badly used, it could no longer keep up with its pack. So it had come to Hawk's cabin. What dim memory, Hawk wondered, had told this wolf it might find succor at a human's dwelling? Had an Indian or a lone trapper once thrown it a bone or let it creep to his fireside and join in a meager supper? Or was it simply sheer desperation, that and the smell of wood smoke from Hawk's chimney?

Whatever had brought it, it was here.

Perhaps Hawk should end the wolf's misery with a well-placed bullet. It would be a kindness. Even if the wolf survived its wounds, it would be fit only to scavenge or live off the leavings of any human who might befriend it—a sorry end for such a magnificent animal.

Hawk went back inside and returned with his rifle. The wolf took one look at the rifle and began to push himself painfully backward through the grass. Appalled at what he had been contemplating, Hawk flung the rifle down. The wolf halted its retreat, its tongue lolling, its ears alert, waiting warily.

Hawk left the wolf and came back out with a fistful of jerky and threw it down in front of the wolf. Famished, it pounced on the meat. In a few quick, growling snaps of the wolf's powerful jaws, the meal vanished. Picking up his rifle, Hawk hurried back into the cabin, left the door open, and lit every lamp. After dropping more jerky on the floor just inside the doorway, he took his reata down from the wall and opened its loop. What he planned would be dangerous, but it was worth a try.

It was not long before the wolf appeared in the doorway, peering in at the jerky. In a chair by the doorway, Hawk waited patiently. It took close to a quarter of an hour for the wolf to move inside the cabin and take the bait.

As the wolf's jaws snapped shut over the jerky, Hawk slipped the reata's noose around its snout, snapping shut the powerful jaws as he dropped onto the wolf's back. For a hairy second or two, the wolf squirmed and lunged about frantically in an effort to dislodge Hawk. Swiftly Hawk wound the reata about the wolf's powerful jaws, then tied its front legs together, immobilizing it completely.

Slamming the door shut, Hawk went to work.

Using soap and water, he cleaned out the wounds thoroughly, then with a pair of shears snipped off inflamed, festering tissue. He found the lacerations even deeper than he had expected, and at one point he had to push back in a small, shiny length of intestine. When he was sure the wounds were as clean as he could get them, he took out his largest needle and best fishing tackle and sewed the wolf up.

The operation concluded, Hawk tore a bedsheet into strips and wound them tightly about the animal's belly, then carried it outside. Driving a stake into the ground, he looped one end of the reata around the wolf's neck, the other around the stake, and left the wolf there.

Exhausted, Hawk returned to his bed.

It was past dawn when he awoke. The first thing he did was check on the wolf. It was gone. Somehow the wolf had worked the reata off its snout, then gnawed through the rawhide tying its two paws together. After that, one snap of its jaw would have been all it took to sever the line holding it.

With a shrug, Hawk retrieved what remained of his reata and went back inside. He doubted he would ever see the wolf again.

* * *

A week later, as he was finishing up the rear shed he had built for his horses, he heard a rustle in the bushes behind him. He turned and saw the wolf trotting slowly out of the timber toward him. It was not limping and it no longer appeared to be in pain.

Some of the torn strips of bedsheet Hawk had used for bandages still clung to it, but most had been gnawed off. A short length of the line Hawk had tied around its neck hung down in front. Once the wolf saw that Hawk had seen it, it pulled up and sat down alertly, its tongue lolling. It seemed to be waiting for a proper invitation to come closer, and Hawk could almost swear it was smiling.

And that made sense. Hawk was smiling, too.

He hurried into the cabin and returned with a fistful of jerky and flung it on the ground in front of the animal. The wolf trotted closer, its eyes on Hawk, hesitated a moment, then flopped down and began eating it. Hawk was close enough to the wolf to untie the line from its neck. He could have patted the wolf on the head if he had wanted, but decided not to do so. Though he would be glad to accept the wolf as a friend, he had no intention of turning him into a pet.

Late one afternoon a week later, Hawk was chopping firewood when the wolf got to its feet and looked down the slope, a low, warning growl coming from deep within its throat.

Hawk let the blade of his ax bite deep into the chopping block and turned, reaching for his rifle as he did so. He relaxed at once. Ben Bluebelly, his long

Kentucky rifle resting across the pommel, was riding up the slope toward him, his pack mule following on a long lead. Glad to see the mountain man, Hawk waved.

Ben had gotten the name "Bluebelly" because of the elaborate bluish tattoo of a grizzly on his stomach. The grizzly's mouth was open, its tongue and canine teeth very much in evidence. Ben had learned how to activate the salivating beast by rippling the appropriate belly muscles, an accomplishment that had done much to strengthen his reputation among the Crow women he preferred. He was wearing a filthy sheepskin coat, buckskin britches, and an ermine cap with long earflaps, which he wore down summer and winter. An old patched buffalo cape was slung over his shoulders.

He glanced uneasily at the wolf as he dismounted. "Got yourself a timber wolf, have you?" he remarked. "It's a big one. What do you call it?"

"I don't call it anything. It isn't a tame house dog. It must've tangled with a wolverine. Got torn up bad. I did what I could for it and now it's keeping close. I don't mind. It's company.

"What brings you this far, Ben?"

"Two reasons." Ben reached into a shirt pocket under his sheepskin and withdrew an envelope. "Here's the first one," he said. "A letter from your sister."

Hawk snatched it from Ben, excused himself with a quick mutter, and tore open the envelope. He read through the letter once quickly, then read the letter more slowly a second time. His first hurried reading told him all that he needed to know. Annabelle was happy. She was getting to like Cambridge, though of course she missed him and wished he would visit her. Her husband, Captain James Merriwether, added a few words, urging him to join them for a visit the coming Christmas. He assured Hawk they would be delighted to have him.

Hawk folded the letter. "Thanks, Ben. That was real decent of you to come all this way to deliver this."

"Glad to do it, Hawk. Linus and Dick knew you'd want to get it soon as possible."

"How is Dick?"

"He looks a mite thin and pale. But that new Flathead squaw of his is treating him real well. Maybe that's why it's taking him so long to get his strength back."

Hawk started down the slope with Ben. "I got a fire roaring inside and there's a full coffeepot sizzling on the mantel. Will you stay the night?"

"Sleep under a roof? Why, sure, Hawk, I'd be much obliged."

"You've had a long ride. Go on inside and I'll tend to your horse and mule."

"God hasn't made you my slave yet," Ben drawled. "I'll see to my own animals, if you promise to keep between me and that wolf of yours. It gets bigger every time I look."

A venison stew was cooking in a huge pot over the fire. Swimming about in the heavy broth, along with the thick chunks of venison, were peeled and sliced potatoes, bits of salt pork, and freshly picked greens.

While the cabin filled with the mouth-watering aroma, Hawk and Ben were nursing their second cup of coffee.

"All right, Ben," Hawk said abruptly. "Out with it."

"Out with what?"

"You said there were two reasons for your riding all this way. Annabelle's letter was one. What's the other?"

Ben pursed his lips thoughtfully, then said, "First off, Hawk, you got anything to sweeten this coffee?"

Hawk retrieved a bottle of whiskey from a wooden box beside the fireplace, unstoppered it, and poured some into Ben's coffee as well as his own. Then he slammed the bottle down on the table and fixed his eyes on Ben.

"I'm still waiting, Ben."

Ben drank half his medicine, then wiped his mouth with the back of his hand. "Hawk, have you noticed anything lately?"

"What the hell kind of question is that, Ben? I been noticing a pile of things lately."

"What I mean is, have you seen any strangers poking around? Any smoke on the horizon?"

"Get to it, Ben."

"Dick wanted me to warn you. He's been hearing things, and so have I."

"I'm losing my patience, Ben."

Ben cleared his throat unhappily. "Before I left the fort, Dick told me how you got that gold those fellows stole from you. He said you found it in Pete Foxwell's saddlebag after he died."

"That's how it happened, Ben."

"I ain't questioning it, Hawk. That isn't why I mentioned it."

"Go on."

"You told Dick Pete stole the gold and hid most of it, but he didn't tell you where. Is that right?"

Hawk nodded.

"But he could've told you if he wanted."

"If he wanted—and if I had asked."

"Which you didn't?"

"Which I didn't."

"Hawk, it's pretty hard to believe Pete Foxwell didn't let on where he'd hid that gold."

"Dammit, Ben! You said you been hearing things. What kind of things?"

"That gang that robbed you at the fort, Hawk. They haven't left for Oregon Territory or any other place. What I been hearing is they're still around, and they're looking for you."

"Me? Why?"

"The way Dick and I figure it, they think you've got more gold than they took from you at the fort."

"That sack of gold coins was all I had."

"I believe you, Hawk. But the thing is, that crew don't believe it."

Hawk sat back in his chair and sipped his coffee. When he saw the intent, worried look on Ben's face, he smiled. "Forget it, Ben. This is big country. Those sailors are just a bunch of greenhorns lost in the middle of it. They're more at home on a rolling deck than out here. Hell, they'll be lucky to survive, let alone find this cabin."

Ben shrugged and leaned back also, seemingly relieved. "That's just what I told Dick. My very words. This ridge is well-hidden and there are no trails leading to it. But Dick wanted me to warn you anyway."

"Don't think I'm not grateful, Ben. I'll be sure to keep my eyes peeled. And thanks again for delivering Annabelle's letter."

"Hawk," Ben remarked, turning about in his chair to look over at the fireplace, "that stew sure smells good. Isn't it about ready yet?"

Hawk walked over to the fireplace and stirred the stew with a long-handled wooden spoon, then lifted a portion of the steaming broth to his lips and sipped carefully. With a pleased smile, he turned to Ben.

"Yes, Ben. It's ready."

The two men dined heartily and with gusto. After the meal, Hawk fed the wolf. Then they lit their pipes and sat out in front of the cabin. As they smoked, they gossiped and swapped stories of trappers they both knew, not forgetting to review the current state of the rivalry between the Rocky Mountain Fur Company and Hudson's Bay.

Nothing more was said about Foxwell's gold or Captain Smollett and his crew.

It was night. Restless, Hawk left his bed, passed Ben Bluebelly, who was snoring quietly on the spare cot, and stepped outside. Walking away from the cabin, he came to rest finally on a log near the woodpile and looked up at the star-flecked sky. A pine-scented breeze swept down from the snow-clad peaks, cooling him. Out of the gloom came the wolf. It halted a few feet from Hawk and flopped down, watching Hawk closely, its ears alert. It was wondering, no doubt, what in blazes Hawk was doing out of his bed at this hour.

Hawk wasn't sure he knew himself. All he knew was he couldn't sleep, and that, despite his words to Ben, he was troubled by the news Ben had brought him. It had been months since any Comanche brave had tried to gain renown and everlasting fame by lifting his scalp. But it was not Commanches Hawk was thinking of now. Not wishing to alarm Ben, Hawk had spoken with more confidence than he had felt. This was big country, all right, but not nearly big enough to elude men like Smollett and his crew.

Earlier that same day Hawk had seen smoke from a campfire. It had been at least a dozen miles distant and came from the direction of Blue Water Pass, a cut that many settlers heading west were now using. But the smoke had come not from a wagon train, but from a single campfire. It could have come from an Indian's fire, or that of a lone trapper. But that was unlikely, for neither would be so lax as to allow such an easily sighted plume of smoke to mark his camp. Only a careless party of white greenhorns would be capable of such a lack of caution.

There was something else. Only Hawk had known that the sack of coins in his possession was but a small portion of the gold taken by Pete Foxwell. Though Hawk had revealed this to Dick Wootton, he had certainly not done so to anyone else at the fort. Yet Smollett evidently knew not only where Hawk's pouch of gold coins had come from, but also that there was much more gold yet to be found. This could mean that the posse that had pursued Pete Foxwell from Taos had not been a posse at all.

But a crew of cutthroats led by one Captain John Smollett.

— 4 —

Digger Finch ducked back out of the blind man's reach.

"Damn you, Digger." the old man cried. "Damn you all to hell!"

As Tim Prew groped for Digger, his leather cape slipped off his shoulders. From under his stocking cap, his snow-white hair stuck out in wild disarray, and his hollow-cheeked face showed the fierce anger he felt.

"Don't get your balls in an uproar, Tim. You aren't any good to us before it gets dark—that's the long and the short of it."

Unable to grab hold of Digger, Tim slumped back on the boulder, his powerful, bony hands trembling violently as they clamped his hickory stick. "Oh, if I had sight for a minute—just one minute," he cried. It was a favorite lament of his.

Digger, well out of his reach, shrugged. "But I've got to admit it, Tim. Once it's dark, you're as good as a sighted man. But you haven't any cause to worry. We won't leave you up here. Not for long, anyway."

"But suppose I wander off and get lost? This ain't like a ship, where a man knows every deck and bulkhead, every sheet and mast. This here is a terrible, fearful wilderness with roots, trees, and bears!"

"I told you. The captain won't leave you behind."

"You bet he won't! Because I'm as good as any one of you."

"There maybe won't be any fighting, Tim. That Hawk feller doesn't even know we're up here. One well-aimed shot and he'll be a dead man. And Foxwell, too, if he's down there."

"I don't care! I'm not staying up here. You tell the captain that!"

"Why don't you tell him yourself?"

"I can't see him! I don't know where he is. You know where he is, so you tell him."

"The captain's busy now. I'm not going to bother him."

Tim snatched up his stick and swung it wildly at Digger. Digger ducked low and remained absolutely still. Whipping the hickory stick back and forth, Tim plunged on past Digger. Digger took after the blind man, caught him from behind, and pushed toward a low ridge of boulders. As the blind man tumbled forward over them, Digger snatched the hickory stick out of his grasp.

"Digger," Tim cried, "give me back my cane."

"Your weapon, you mean."

On his hands and knees the blind man began searching the ground, frantic to find the hickory stick. "Where is it?" he wailed. "What have you done with it?"

"I got it," Digger told him. "I'll give it back. But the next time you come at me with it, I'll ram it up your ass."

"All right, Digger," Tim said. "Just give it back."

Digger reached over and placed the weapon into the blind man's grasp. Grasping it quickly, Tim sat up and pulled his leather cape over his shoulders. His anger was gone. Instead, the old man appeared subdued. Digger felt sorry for him.

"Don't fret," he told Tim. "I'll go see the captain."

"Just tell him I don't want to be left up here alone." Tim's voice almost broke. "It's bears I'm afraid of most, Digger. Bears!"

Digger crossed over the rocky spine to where the captain was talking to Big Tom and Joe Red Feather, the half-breeds who had been acting as scouts, looking for this Hawk fellow's cabin. Two days ago they had come into camp with good news. The captain's search was over. The two breeds had found Hawk's cabin. If luck was with them, they had found Foxwell and the rest of the gold.

They were now on a ridge high above the lubber's cabin, getting ready to move on him. Digger glanced down at it. Smoke was rising out from the chimney. They'd caught sight of Hawk coming and going like he was going to live forever. An hour ago he had been working on the roof. Since then he'd been keeping inside. They had not yet caught sight of Foxwell. Digger wasn't surprised at that. Foxwell was dead. No man could live after what they had done to him.

Digger looked back at the captain. Digger knew enough not to interrupt him. He sat down on a log and waited for the captain to finish with the breeds.

". . . so just find out if Foxwell is in there with him," the captain was telling them.

"'How you want us do that?" Big Tom asked.

"Ask Hawk if he's alone," the captain snapped, not bothering to hide his irritation at their stupidity. "Invite yourselves into the cabin. And if you see a chance to take him alive, do it."

Joe Red Feather nodded, glaring back implacably at the captain. He made no effort to hide his feelings for Smollett. He hated all white men as much as he hated Crow, but this captain he despised even more than the white man who had raped his mother. This did not matter now, however. He would take Golden Hawk, and with his famous captive, he would return at last to the lodge of his mother's people, the Pine Lodge Blackfoot. An outcast no longer, he would be famous and lead many war parties against these white faces.

Joe Red Feather nudged Big Tom. "We go now," he told the captain.

The captain watched them mount up and ride out, their belts crowded with pistols and knives, each one packing a long Kentucky rifle. They wore wide-brimmed hats. From under the hat brims their black hair hung in long, gleaming braids clear down to the backs of their filthy frock coats.

The captain turned to Digger. "What do you want, Digger?"

"Tim wants to go down with us."

"I already told him to stay up here. He'll be swinging at trees with that damned cane of his.

And if we give him a gun, he'll likely kill one of us."

"He just don't want to be left up here alone, Captain."

"Why not?"

"He's afraid we'll leave him for good."

"Might be a damned good idea. He's getting to be a nuisance."

"You wouldn't do that, Captain."

"Why not?"

"The men wouldn't stand for it."

"They'll bloody well stand for anything I tell them to stand for—and that goes for you too, Digger."

Ignoring the threat, Digger said, "Tim's afraid of bears, too."

The captain's face softened. "I don't blame him. Those grizzlies, especially. All right. We'll take him down with us. But I'm making him your responsibility, Digger. You keep him the hell out of our way."

"I'll do what I can, sir."

"You do better than that. If you don't control him, cut the old bastard's throat and be done with it."

"Thank you, Captain."

As Digger turned and walked back to Tim, the captain walked over to the lip of the ridge and peered down at the cabin. Mr. Hawk, if that was his name, was still inside and had been for close to an hour. Most of the morning he had been applying a heavy layer of mud to the roof. The breeds seemed to think he was expecting an attack, that the mud was there to protect the roof from fire arrows. If so, this meant he knew that the captain and his crew were about to pay him a visit.

As he watched, the two breeds broke from the timber and continued down the slope toward the cabin. A moment later Hawk appeared in the cabin doorway. Beside him appeared the huge wolf they had all noticed. He was carrying a rifle. The breeds halted and dismounted, holding their hands up in the traditional sign for peace.

When Hawk beckoned them closer, the captain smiled.

Hawk had recognized the breeds at once. The tallest was Joe Red Feather. His companion was Big Tom. They hung about Fort Hall usually, sometimes bringing in fresh venison for the fort or hiring out as guides for settlers eager for shortcuts to the Oregon Territory. They always seemed to return sooner than they should have from such errands, and there were rumors that they were not all wise in their choice of trails, and that any wagonmasters who relied on them as guides became singularly unlucky. For the past six months or so the two had been absent from the fort and everyone who knew them had breathed easier.

Hawk did not trust them. He was almost certain they were working with the captain now, reconnoitering the cabin to see if he were alone. As the two walked closer, the wolf darted from his side toward them. Hawk did not call the wolf back. The breeds tried to ignore the big wolf as he circled them, his teeth bared.

"Call off this wolf," Joe Red Feather said, halting. "What do you want?"

"We are tired," Big Tom said. "We like fresh tobacco, some food, maybe."

"Don't come any closer."

Hawk slipped back into his cabin, reappearing a moment later with a small pouch of tobacco and strips of jerky. He walked out to the Indians and handed it to them.

"You can build a fire over there," Hawk told them, pointing to a spot under some pines.

Joe Red Feather glanced past Hawk at the open cabin doorway. "Are you alone?"

"Why do you want to know?"

The breed shrugged, a leaden insolence in his eyes. "If you're alone, you have plenty room, could share your lodge with us."

Hawk smiled coldly at the half-breed. "Like I just told you, build a fire over there and stay out here for the night. Don't come any closer to my cabin, and I'll expect you to pull out first thing in the morning."

"Is this white man's hospitality?"

Without answering, Hawk returned to the cabin, pausing in the open doorway to look back at the breeds. As he had expected, they had no reason to accept a hospitality so grudgingly and meanly offered. They mounted up and rode off. As they rode off toward the timber, the wolf trotted back to Hawk, who stepped aside to let him in. Then he shut the door.

Since Ben Blueberry's warning, he had been busy turning the cabin into a fortress. In order to allow himself to lay flat while he fired out at any attackers, he had knocked holes in the chinking between the logs close to the floor. He had just finished covering the roof with a layer of mud, and under the floor's rough planking he had dug out a cellar and constructed small trapdoors from which he could fire up at anyone storming into the cabin. In case he had to give it up and flee, he had dug out a short tunnel that led from the cellar to a clump of bushes behind the cabin.

As a final precaution, he had left his two pack horses and his saddle horses in an isolated stream-watered valley three miles distant. The pack horses had been laden with supplies, more than enough to provide for Hawk if he were forced to flee any distance. The day before he had checked on the three horses and found their hobbles still secure, the stream providing them with more than adequate water.

He was as ready as he would ever be for an assault on what he had come to regard as his citadel.

It was Joe Red Feather who told Smollett of the cairn he and Big Tom had discovered on their way back from the cabin.

Smollett had promptly left his men and, accompanied by Blackie and Bim Wheeler, had hurried over to examine the neat pile of stones and fair-sized boulders. It was undoubtedly of recent construction. He directed Blackie and Dick to pull it down.

They did so promptly, scattering the cairn's boulders over the small clearing, the breeds watching fearfully. When the two men began poking clumsily about in the uncovered grave, the breeds retreated to the woods bordering the clearing. Smollett had no such compunctions. He peered closely over the men's shoulders as they dug clumsily at the gravesite with their rifle stocks.

A heavy clod of dirt was knocked aside. Smollett gasped. He was looking into the eye sockets of a corpse. The stench was awful, but there was enough left of the man's face and clothing for him to assure himself that this rotting piece of flesh had once been Pete Foxwell. Backing away hastily, Smollett turned and hurried back to his waiting men.

"Keep going on down this mountain," he told them. "Foxwell's dead for sure. He was just staring up at me out of hell. All we got to deal with now is that Hawk fellow down there."

As Smollett picked his way down the slope with his men, he went over in his mind what he had long suspected must have happened. Pete Foxwell had managed to get to Hawk's cabin and, once there, had died of his wounds. That explained where Hawk got the gold he was flashing in Fort Hall.

Which meant the rest of the gold was here, somewhere. Either in the cabin or buried close by. All they had to do was catch that fellow inside the cabin and make him tell. If he refused, the breeds would step in. Smollett had heard some pretty hair-raising accounts of what some Indians could do to a white man.

Smollett and his men reached the clearing on which the cabin sat. The cabin was at its farthest edge, close under a towering mountain flank, the clearing itself completely surrounded by timber.

His men crouching behind him, Smollett peered at the cabin over a low saddle of ground. It was about one hundred yards away. Hawk was evidently still inside the cabin. Wood smoke was rising out of the chimney.

The captain had decided to make his approach while it was still light. He had spoken to this fellow at the fort; now they would talk again. Smollett would simply point out that there was no sense in prolonging matters. They were both reasonable men. If Hawk was willing to give up peaceably, there did not have to be any bloodshed. After all, this gold did not belong to him. It was Foxwell's gold—stolen gold.

It belonged to anyone who was strong enough to take it—and keep it.

Smollett turned to wave on his men. They followed him up onto the saddleback and across the clearing toward the cabin, a ragged, mean-looking crew, each man's weapon cocked and ready. When they were about halfway to the cabin, its door opened and Hawk stepped out, a rifle in his hand, a pistol in his belt. Beside him stood the wolf, as big as Big Tom and Joe Red Feather had said he was.

Smollett was pleased. The fellow could have cut him down with a single shot. But he hadn't. He was willing to talk. Smollett could sense this in the way the man looked past the small army of armed men flanking him. He knew when he was licked.

The wolf had long since warned Hawk of the presence of Smollett and his crew, and Hawk had begun to wonder what was keeping them. He was not surprised when he saw Joe Red Feather and Big Tom among Smollett's crew.

Hawk lifted his rifle to train it on Smollett. "You better stop right there, Captain."

"I want to talk. Let me come closer."

"Come ahead. But tell your men to stay where they are."

The captain spoke briefly to his men, then continued on to the cabin. Hawk snapped his fingers at the wolf, who promptly flopped down beside him. As he drew within a few yards, Smollett glanced nervously at the animal.

"Hold it, Captain."

The captain halted. Alerted by Hawk's tone, the wolf rose up onto all fours.

"What do you and your cutthroats want, Smollett?"

"Hell, guv'nor, you mean you don't know?"

"Gold."

"That's what I like," Smollett said, "a man who says what's on his mind without dilly-dallying around. A man after my own heart, sir, and that's a fact."

"Get on with it, Captain."

"You said it's gold we want, and that's the pure and simple truth of this business here and now."

"I don't have it."

"Come, now, gov'nor. That gold we took from you in Fort Hall came from the same chest of gold coins Foxwell took. Don't deny it."

"Who's denying it?"

"Then how do you expect me to believe you don't have the rest of the gold in that cabin behind you?"

"Foxwell took it with him when he left."

Smollett smiled. "Foxwell is dead. I just saw his rotting corpse, up there on the hill where you laid him to rest. Foxwell reached here before he died. Now, why don't you make it simple for yourself and hand it over to me?"

"I don't have it, Smollett. Foxwell hid the gold before he got here."

"You expect me to believe that?"

"I don't care what you believe, Smollett."

"Let my men search your cabin."

"Go ahead. Search all you like."

The captain rubbed his stubbly chin with the back of his hand, his eyes narrowing. "All right. So the gold ain't in there. You've hid it out here somewhere."

As far as Hawk was concerned, the debate was over. He had made an effort to convince Smollett he did not have the gold, and had been caught in a lie for his trouble. There was nothing more he could do. For a moment he considered holding Smollett hostage. But he doubted such a move would give him any real leverage with this crew of blackguards. After due consideration, they wouldn't give a damn what happened to Smollett. And besides, it would be difficult enough to keep track of the captain's men without having to deal with the captain at the same time.

Hawk waggled his rifle. "Turn around and start walking, Smollett."

"You won't reconsider?"

"Move! Before I sic the wolf on you."

Smollett turned hastily and hurried back toward his men.

Hawk stepped back inside the cabin and slapped his thigh to bring the wolf back in with him. After closing the door, he slid a rough two-by-four across it, then watched from his window as the captain and his crew moved back across the clearing.

Come dark, the captain's men would likely attack. But Smollett had a problem. He could not allow his men to go completely wild, to pull out every stop. He needed to capture Hawk alive—for as far as he knew only Hawk could take him to the gold.

Hawk left the window and began his preparations for nightfall.

— 5 —

As soon as it was dark, Hawk let the wolf out.

Before dusk, he had seen the captain's men drifting down through the timber, preparing to rush the cabin when night closed in. Earlier, two rifle shots had slammed into the door. Though they were intended to intimidate Hawk, they simply forewarned him.

He left the cabin by his hidden rear tunnel, ducked through the bushes, and ran for the timber. Once there, he waited. Not long after, a scream broke the silence. Then he heard the low, ferocious growling of the wolf. It had found one of the captain's men skulking in the timber and was attacking. Hawk listened and shuddered. He did not envy the man.

He moved closer to the sound of the struggle, keeping close to the edge of the timber. A man ran into the clearing, the wolf on his heels. Raising his rifle, Hawk tracked the running man and squeezed the trigger. He stumbled once, then plunged into the dark ground and lay still.

The wolf ran back into the timber. Almost at

once another cry came from the darkness as a second man fled the timber, this one heading almost straight at Hawk. Stepping out of cover, Hawk raised his revolver and fired point-blank. The fleeing man dropped.

Again the wolf spun about and headed back into the timber. It never got there. A crash of rifle fire brought it down. The wolf went flying, jumped up, and dragged itself into the timber.

Someone crashed through the brush behind Hawk. He turned in time to see a tall fellow—wielding what appeared to be a short, flat sword—coming at him full tilt. Hawk ducked low. The fellow charged past him in the darkness, confused. Hawk spun and came down on the man's head with the butt of his revolver. The fellow collapsed, vanishing into the brush.

Hawk turned. The rifle shot that brought down the wolf had come from behind the cabin. Reloading his Hawken as he ran, he circled around the cabin and came out behind the breed, Big Tom. He was crouched at the corner of the cabin, facing the moonlit clearing. At Hawk's approach he spun about. Hawk threw himself to the ground. The half-breed swung up his ancient pistol and fired. The round missed. Hawk fired back. His shot, too, went wild. Big Tom unsheathed his knife and charged. Planting his bowie blade up into the ground, Hawk waited until Big Tom threw himself at Hawk, then rolled away. The big half-breed came down hard, impaling himself on the upturned blade. His startled, despairing cry filled the night.

Snatching up his rifle, Hawk ran for the cabin doorway. One of the captain's men raced out of the darkness to cut him off. Hawk reached the door first, pulled it open, then stepped aside, pulling the door open wider. His pursuer bolted past him into the cabin. Hawk slammed the door shut and flung the beam across it.

Then he turned to face his pursuer.

The only light came from the fire in the fireplace. In its red glow he could see that this fellow was sure as hell big enough. His head was wrapped in a dirty red bandanna and he held a long dagger, pirate-fashion, in his teeth.

He grinned at Hawk and plucked the blade from his mouth. "The captain wants you alive, but I seen what you done to my mates. I'm going to carve your liver and make you eat it."

He lunged for Hawk. Hawk ducked aside as the big fellow's knife nearly decapitated him. Again the pirate's knife sliced dangerously close as it snicked past Hawk's cheek. But the pirate's enthusiasm caused him to throw caution to the winds and lost his balance.

Before he could regain it, Hawk flung his rifle, barrel first, into the man's gut. It slammed deep, clear to his backbone. The big fellow doubled over, clutching at his midsection with both hands. He hit the floor and began to writhe in agony.

Hawk walked over to inspect him. He was still conscious. Hawk picked up his knife, ripped off his bandanna, and with the point of his knife sliced a neat line around his hairline. With a quick, snapping motion, Hawk lifted the seaman's scalp. After stuffing the bloody trophy into the man's side pocket, he opened the door and dragged him outside.

Through a gun port Hawk watched, waiting to see how many more there would be to try their luck with him. Someone dashed out of the night to drag away the scalped pirate. After that came four or five shots into the cabin's walls and door. Another spiteful flurry took out the windows. Then silence.

How many of the captain's men did he take out? Hawk wondered. Big Tom, for one. The two others he shot outside. Another he clubbed. And now this one. Hawk was making them think twice about taking him alive. But the cost had been high. The wolf had been hit. How bad, he didn't know. Hawk felt an angry emptiness.

He had come to appreciate the wolf's silent, independent companionship.

Smollett dropped down behind the ridge, his men streaming after him. In the dim light that came from the splinter of a moon overhead, he could see their grim, ashen faces. Not a man who had seen Jamie's bloody, scalped skull remained unshaken. Will Hollings and Bim Wheeler were dead, and Henry Tice had been clubbed senseless and was still babbling incoherently. Smollett saw Joe Red Feather jump down behind the ridge alone—and realized that the breed's comrade was most likely gone too.

Smollett sighed wearily. The only good thing was that they had gotten rid of the wolf.

"We better burn that blighter out," Digger said.

"Too risky," snapped Smollett. "We'd burn him up too, and then where would we be?"

"Hell, we ain't getting nowhere this way."

"What I'd like to know," someone else grumbled, "is how he got out of that cabin in the first place."

"He must've slipped out when he let the wolf loose."

"If he did, none of us saw it."

"It was too dark."

"Goddammit, I say we burn him out," repeated Digger.

Ignoring Digger, the captain peered over the ridge at the cabin. Hawk had not lit any lanterns; the windows were dark. How *had* the son of a bitch managed to slip out? Well, they'd just have to see he stayed inside until he starved. He couldn't live in there forever, not without food and water, he couldn't.

The captain told his men they were going to keep the cabin surrounded until the son of a bitch inside surrendered—no matter how long it took. Some of his men looked relieved. They had been afraid the captain's impatience might cause him to order a frontal assault.

Hawk slept through the next day by constantly prodding himself awake to look for any sign that the captain's forces might be moving against him. At the far end of the clearing behind a low ridge, a steady column of smoke arose from a campfire, marking Smollett's camp. There had been no movement in the timber close to the cabin all day. But no more potshots had been taken at it.

The more he thought about it, the more certain Hawk became that Smollett would now try to starve him out.

As soon as it was dark enough, Hawk ducked out of the cabin's rear exit and visited his three horses. They were skittish and nearly out of graze. He moved them to another spot farther downstream, then filled three canteens and returned to the cabin.

As long as he could continue to supply himself with fresh water, he knew he could hold out indefinitely. He had enough salt pork, jerky, and potatoes for a month long siege—and longer if it came to that.

It was past midnight and the captain was finding it difficult to sleep. Puffing forlornly on his pipe, he stared bleakly into the fire.

Things were not going well.

He was sitting on a folded blanket just outside the campfire's ring of light. All about him in the darkness, sleeping forms were dimly visible. Despite Smollett's pleas, his men were losing heart. The sight of Jamie's scalped head—and the way he had to walk around painfully doubled over—had considerably dimmed their enthusiasm for this siege, which had already lasted more than a week. Indeed, Smollett was coming to realize he was dealing with men dangerously close to mutiny.

Joe Red Feather materialized out of the darkness and hunkered down beside Smollett. The captain took the pipe out of his mouth. "What do you want, Joe?"

"Golden Hawk has another way out of his cabin."

Smollett turned to stare at Joe Red Feather. "What's that, Joe?"

The breed almost smiled at the captain's response. "At night Golden Hawk use a tunnel back of his cabin to get water and maybe fresh game."

"Jesus, Joe! You sure of this?"

"I'll take you to the tunnel. Maybe you can send someone through it into the cabin while the others storm the cabin. Then maybe siege will be over."

Smollett was so pleased at this news he almost slapped the Indian on the back. He stood quickly, already certain whom he'd be sending into the cabin through the back entrance. Old Tim Prew. In that darkness, the blind old son of a bitch would be as good as any sighted man. Maybe even better.

"Stay put," Smollett told the half-breed, "while I wake these damn no-accounts."

Angry grumbling filled the air as Smollett roused his men. But once they heard Joe Red Feather's news, they quieted, picked up their weapons, and let the breed lead them through the timber.

Once they came out at the rear of the cabin, Joe Red Feather pointed out a thick clump of bushes hard against the cabin's backside. Smollett pulled back the bushes and peered down at the tunnel entrance. In the moonlight he could see the entrance clearly. Apparently, the tunnel led under the cabin into a shallow cellar or crawl space. Glowing embers in the cabin's fireplace was the source of the cabin's only light. For the past week, Smollett's men had amused themselves by taking potshots at what was left of the windows and there was now not a single pane left.

Smollett motioned to Digger to bring Tim Prew closer. When the two got close enough to the bushes, Digger parted the tangle of branches and let Tim cock his ear at the entrance.

"He's in there," Tim said after a moment. "I can hear him sleeping. Son of a bitch snores."

Smollett sure as hell found that hard to believe, but he said nothing.

"You better be careful now," Digger told Tim. "He's a mean one."

Patting the knife sheathed at his waist, Tim grinned. "Don't you worry none about me."

Smollett leaned close to the blind man. "All you got to do is distract the son of a bitch while we rush the cabin. Don't use that knife unless you have to. The blighter ain't no good to us dead."

"I know that, Captain. We all want our share of that gold."

The captain turned to Digger. "Stay close by here in case Tim needs help."

"You want me to go in with him?"

"No. Just keep that lubber from breaking out."

Digger took out his pistol. He would be ready enough if this Hawk fellow popped his head out. There was enough of a moon to give him plenty of light. Of course, he wouldn't kill the lubber, he'd just wound him.

Unless he had no choice.

Hawk awakened suddenly. Fingers were fluttering over his face like the wings of a moth. A second later the needle-sharp tip of a blade was pressed with quick, cruel precision into the flesh under his Adam's apple, and he smelled the sour breath of the man crouching over him in the darkness. As the knife's pressure increased, he was forced relentlessly down onto the floor.

He had fallen asleep on the floor just inside the door. Earlier, he had thrown enough wood on the fire to give the cabin light. But its interior was now as black as the inside of an inkwell. Whoever was pressing the blade into his throat must have thrown water on the fire.

"I got him!" the man atop him cried.

His full weight was on Hawk's chest, his sharp knees digging into the upper portion of his arms, pinning them to the floor. As he pressed the point of his knife deeper into Hawk's throat, he cried out a second time. "Hurry it up, you blighters!"

Hawk realized his escape tunnel had been discovered. And this tough little son of a bitch on top of him had entered through it while he slept. Hawk was certain he had heard the man's voice before. Peering closely up at the man's profile, he saw it was the blind man he had tangled with at Fort Hall, the one who had stabbed Dick Wootton.

From outside came the pounding of feet heading for the cabin. When the first of the captain's men reached it, he tried to slam through the door, but the beam across the door held. Another man struck it, shoulder down, but still the door would not yield.

"Get a battering ram," someone cried.

"No," Hawk heard the captain insist. "Boost someone in through the window."

What remained of the sash was yanked from the window on the other side of the door. A gun barrel cleared away the remaining glass shards. Hawk saw the head and shoulders of someone boosting himself through the opening a moment before he dropped into the cabin. The knife at Hawk's throat dug deeper as the blind man sitting on Hawk's chest shifted his weight slightly to shift toward the sound of the one who had just entered.

Completely relaxed, offering no resistance, Hawk had been waiting for this moment. He flung his thighs upward, momentarily dislodging the blind man. A second before his knife clattered to the floor, Hawk felt it dig cruelly into his throat.

Ignoring the pain, Hawk grabbed the blind man's arms and flung him over his head. As the man struck the floor behind Hawk, Hawk jumped to his feet, snatched up one of his chairs, and shattered it over the head of the fellow who had just come through the window. The man sank to the floor and Hawk heard the blind man rushing him from behind.

Hawk spun, sweeping his other chair around in time to catch him chest-high. The blind man struck the chair with the force and fury of a thunderbolt. His legs went flying out from under him and he skidded past Hawk all the way to the wall, where he remained on his back, groaning loudly. Another of the captain's men boosted himself through the window. Grabbing his rifle, Hawk slammed its stock full in the man's face, knocking him back out through the window.

There was a momentary lull. Those outside knew that he was wide awake now, fully aroused, and that the blind man had failed to restrain him.

Hawk tied his shirt around his waist, fumbled under his cot for his revolver and stuck it into his belt. Then he dropped through a trapdoor into the cellar. On his hands and knees, he pushed himself along until he felt the cool night air gently buffeting his face. There had to be someone waiting for him when he poked his head out. But all he could do was keep going.

Reaching the tunnel's mouth, he lay flat and peered out at the dark bushes crowding it, waiting until his eyes adjusted to the dim, moonlit tangle of branches. A dark form materialized just behind the bushes, then parted them. A man's head poked through, his face clearly visible to Hawk.

Then the man saw Hawk. "Tim? That you? It's Digger! What's happening?"

Hawk reached up and caught Digger behind the neck. Slamming the man's head brutally down through the bushes, Hawk vaulted out of the tunnel, crashed through the bushes, and headed for the timber.

Another of the captain's men came at him from his left. Still running full tilt, Hawk spun completely around, the stock of his rifle smashing the fellow under his chin. With a strangled cry, the man sagged to the ground, both hands clasping his throat.

A second later Hawk was in the timber, plunging through the awesome darkness. He narrowly missed some trees and slammed into others. Behind him came shouts and cries, even a flurry of rifle fire. But the sound of pursuit faded rapidly. Nevertheless, Hawk did not slow as he headed for the valley where he had left the horses.

He stumbled on a tree root and sprawled headlong. When he could not spring immediately back up onto his feet, he noticed the slick, warm shield of blood covering his chest. He reached up with his hand to feel his throat wound and discovered how deep that last thrust of the blind man's knife had gone.

Out through the ragged hole—in short, powerful bursts—Hawk's racing heart was pumping out his lifeblood.

— 6 —

Sprinkling gunpowder over a patch cloth, Hawk pushed a corner of it into the neck wound until the bleeding stopped. Ignoring how fiercely it stung, he leaned his head back against a tree and closed his eyes. He remembered little else until he awoke the next morning to the first rays of the sunlight slanting through the timber.

From the sun's position Hawk reckoned it to be almost seven o'clock. He looked down at his chest. The dried blood had crusted. He had stopped the bleeding. His throat throbbed steadily and he was aware that if he removed the patch cloth the bleeding might start up again. Kicking off a boot, he wound a sock tightly about his neck to keep the patch cloth in place.

His head reeling, he struggled to his feet. Until the ground grew solid under his feet once more, he held on to a tree, then started off. When he reached the valley, he found his horses in fine condition, if a little skittish. After loading up the pack horses, he saddled his mount. He had to sit down for a while after this exertion, and by the time he was able to mount up, he was again close to passing out.

Not long after, cresting a pine-studded spur, he glanced back. A thick black column of smoke rose into the morning sky. It was his cabin, he had no doubt. Though he had expected this, the sight of that sad plume of smoke pumping into the morning sky caused his heart to thud angrily. Someday he would make that damned pirate pay for this.

Smollett shaded his eyes from the leaping flames, then glanced up at the smoke pumping skyward. It gave him some satisfaction to see the bastard's cabin going up like this. But he'd be feeling a lot better if he had found in the cabin some indication of where that son of a bitch had hid the gold.

The fact that he and his men had found nothing galled him, filling him with a dark, bitter frustration. They had nearly caught the bastard. Tim's knife had his blood on it. But now he was gone. And with him any chance of finding that gold unless they caught up to him once more and this time beat the truth out of him.

Some of his men had no appetite for continuing what to them appeared to be a fruitless quest. Though Smollett still found this hard to believe, he had heard two of his men discussing the possibility of returning to Frisco to sign on with one of those China clippers—despite the fact that both lubbers were known in every port west of Singapore as mutineers, and worse.

Digger approached, his face a swollen, purplish mess. "Looks like we got company, Captain."

Digger pointed.

Smollett turned around and saw three Indians riding onto the clearing, trailing a small remuda of ponies behind them. They did not resemble at all the filthy blanket Indians Smollett had seen idling around the trading posts. Darkly tanned, their chests and arms covered with colorful stripes, their upper torsos bare except for blankets or buffalo capes thrown over their shoulders, they looked like an entirely new breed of savage. It was apparent they were from a land far south of this high country. They wore headdresses adorned with buffalo horns, imparting to them a fierce, barbaric splendor. Watching them approach, Smollett felt his blood race through his veins.

Joe Red Feather, his eyes alight with both admiration and fear, hurried over to Smollett.

"Who the hell are they, Joe?"

"Comanches. I do not know which band for sure. I think maybe Kwahadi."

"Where are they from?"

"The grasslands below the southern herd. They have come from the high plateau, a hot, dry land. These are fierce warriors, Captain. The Crow are the best horse thieves. But no Crow dares steal a horse from the Comanche."

The men digging all over in search of the gold put down their shovels and moved cautiously closer to watch the approaching Indians. Many were bandaged crudely, and the scalped Jamie still walked bent over like an old man, his head swathed in bandages. The three Comanches rode boldly up to Smollett, then held their hands up, palm outward, in the traditional sign of peace.

Joe Red Feather returned the sign. So did Smollett.

One of the Indians dismounted and advanced toward them. The other two warriors slipped off their ponies also, but remained back with their remuda.

The Comanche approaching the captain was a fierce-looking old bird, but Smollett was surprised how squat and ungainly he and his fellow warriors were. They were flabby about the middle and had severely bowed legs, as if they had spent their entire lives on horseback and were only barely able to function on foot. As the Indian approaching him got closer, Smollett noticed the scar about three inches long above his eyebrow and another that ran down the side of his face clear to his chin.

"You better do the talking, Joe," Smollett said.

"I do not know the Comanche tongue. I will speak with my hands."

The captain watched, fascinated, as Joe Red Feather conversed with the Comanche using only his hands. Their hands moved like lightning, sometimes in flowing, sinuous lines, at other times with sharp, chopping strokes, but always with an exciting grace. Every now and then a few words were exchanged, but for the most part, the two conversed entirely through their hands.

When the Comanche had finished, Joe Red Feather turned to the captain. "These warriors know you chase Golden Hawk. They see now that you have burned his lodge. So they greet you as a brother. They too are after Golden Hawk."

"You mean they know the blighter?"

"Yes. For many years."

"How come?"

"Golden Hawk is also a Comanche. They took him and his sister when they were small. For many years Golden Hawk lived with them as a slave, tending their pony herds. When he escaped, he killed a famous war chief and many others. Now the old chief who makes peace with him is dead, so these Comanches come far to take his scalp or bring him back as their captive."

"This fellow, Golden Hawk, hell, is he really that hard to take?"

The flesh at the corners of Joe Red Feather's eyes crinkled slightly. "You did not find this so, Captain?"

"Yes, dammit, I have," the captain admitted. "Well, then, tell these savages I'll help track that son of a bitch, if that's what they want. But tell them I must have a few words with him before they get their hands on him. He's the only one knows where that gold is, don't forget."

Joe Red Feather conveyed this to the Comanche, who responded quickly. "This chief's all for capturing Golden Hawk alive," Joe said. "He wants to drive Golden Hawk before him when he enters his village. For many moons their women will keep him alive, until they destroy the Hawk's accursed white soul. He says if you're around then, you can ask Golden Hawk anything you want."

"That's fair enough—hell, that's real decent of him."

Joe Red Feather nodded. "But he warns that taking Golden Hawk alive will not be easy. Already Golden Hawk has killed many brave Comanche warriors. Some say he is in league with the Great Cannibal Owl."

"That's bullshit and you know it, Joe."

Joe Red Feather shrugged and turned back to the

Comanche to tell him that Smollett agreed to work together with him to bring in Golden Hawk. With a grunt of agreement, the Comanche spun about to rejoin his companions.

After the Comanches rode off into the timber behind the still-burning cabin, Joe Red Feather turned to the captain. "I told that war chief which way Golden Hawk went. He says you and your men better mount up now and follow him if you want Golden Hawk."

Smollett watched the Comanches disappear into the timber, their eyes searching the ground for sign. They sure as hell weren't wasting any time. He turned to Digger, who had kept himself well back during this parley with the Comanches.

"We're moving out, Digger. Now. Tell the men we got some real Indians this time to track that bastard. All we got to do is keep up with them."

Digger hurried across the clearing to the captain's waiting men. Without a word to Smollett, Joe Red Feather headed toward the ridge on the far end of the clearing.

"Where are you going, Joe?" Smollett asked.

The breed halted and turned to look back at Smollett. He had been stung by that crack about real Indians, but kept his composure. "My horse is already saddled. I want Golden Hawk, too." His impassive face became cold with resolve. "Maybe I get a piece of him, too."

"A piece of him? What the hell for?"

"That is my business, Captain."

Watching Joe Red Feather go, Smollett had the uneasy sense that things were coming unglued. He shook the feeling off and hurried after Digger to get his own things ready.

* * *

Hawk reined in his mount, folded his arms over the pommel, and peered beyond the canyon's rim at the cabin below. A thin trace of wood smoke was rising from its chimney. Its pungent fragrance reminded Hawk how long it had been since he had slept under a roof.

A small barn stood beside the cabin. Behind it, a paint was resting its cheek on the corral's top rail. Several mules were picketed in the pasture beyond the barn, quietly cropping the grass at their feet. In front of the cabin, beaver pelts were stretched on willow frames. From this distance Hawk could tell the plews were from good-sized beavers, weighing in at close to sixty pounds.

It had been the smell of wood smoke that had drawn Hawk to this canyon. Pulling his mount back from the edge, he returned to the game trail he had been following. When the canyon floor came into sight, he gave his mount its head and let it choose its own pace as it picked its way along the precarious trail. His two pack horses were a bit skittish at the beginning of the descent, but they quieted down before long and gave Hawk no trouble. When he reached the floor of the canyon, he was almost a mile beyond the cabin. Doubling back, he reached it just as dusk was falling.

Approaching the cabin, he called, "Hello, the cabin!"

The door opened and Ben Bluebelly stepped out.

"You old son of a bitch," Hawk said. "So this is your place, is it?"

"Guess you found me out, Hawk."

"The smell of your wood smoke fetched me. How about it, Ben? Is there a fire and a pot of hot coffee under it?"

"There sure is, Hawk. Glad for the company."

"I'll just take care of my horses first."

"There's a clean stall and plenty of oats in the barn. The water bucket is inside the door."

"Much obliged."

Hawk dismounted and led his horse toward the barn.

A few minutes later, as he stepped into Ben's cabin, the first thing he noticed was the man lying on a straw mattress close by the wood stove. He had suffered some fearful accident. Torn strips from a wool shirt were wound tightly around his head and face. Only his left eye was visible, and at the spot where his mouth should be, there was a small, discolored hole in the bandage.

Hawk walked over to the table where Ben was placing down two mugs and a pot of coffee. The injured man raised his head, his one eye regarding Hawk closely. Sitting down at the table, Hawk nodded to him. The fellow managed a slight nod in return, then dropped his head back onto the mattress, his one uncovered eye staring at the ceiling.

Ben filled his own mug and then shoved the pot across the table to Hawk. With a flick of his eyes, Hawk indicated the man on the mattress. "What happened to him, Ben?"

"His name's Cy—Cyrus Martin. He's the one brought that paint to me about two weeks ago," Ben replied, making no effort to lower his voice. "Some crazy drunk Mandans caught him unawares and beat on him until they got tired of it. Then they bound his wrists, tied him to that paint out there, and walloped the pony on the backside. He plowed up a lot of landscape before he managed to snag the rawhide around a sapling and halt the pony. Cy was still on the pony's back when he showed up here, his wrists still bound."

"How bad hurt was he?"

"He lost an eye and stove in one side of his face. I set the jaw as best I could, but his cheekbone's gonna have to stay out of place. I thought for a while he was going to lose the remaining eye, but it's healing just fine now. I'm taking off his bandages tomorrow."

"How does he eat if his jaw is broken?"

Ben smiled proudly. "He's drinking plenty of pemmican soup through a hollow reed I got for him." Ben seemed justifiably proud of his efforts on the luckless fellow's behalf.

Hawk finished his coffee and reached for the pot. While he poured, Ben said, "You haven't told me what you're doing this far south, Hawk. Last I knew you were working pretty hard on that cabin of yours."

"It went up in smoke, Ben."

"Was I right, then? Those crazy sailors from Fort Hall caught up with you, did they?"

Hawk nodded.

"I tried to warn you, Hawk."

"And I'm glad you did. When they reached my cabin, I was ready for them. Otherwise, I wouldn't be here now."

"Too bad about your cabin."

Hawk shrugged.

"So what now?"

"I'm heading back to Fort Hall—and taking the long way around."

"You mean you're running from those bastards."

"I need time, Ben—time to make plans. When I catch up to Captain Smollett and his crew next time, I want it to be on my terms."

"Why don't you just tell them where the gold is, Hawk?"

Hawk was astounded. For a moment he could not believe he had heard correctly. "Did I hear you right, Ben?"

"You did. Hawk, dammit, let them have the gold. It's a curse, Hawk. Look what it's done to you already. Get rid of it."

"You still think I know where that gold is buried."

"Well, don't you?"

"Dammit, Ben! What I told you is the truth."

Ben took out his pipe and glanced over the bowl as he pressed fresh tobacco into it. "If that's the way you want it, Hawk . . . I won't say another word."

"I'd sure appreciate that, Ben."

"You stayin' for the night?"

"If you'll have me."

"There's plenty of room, Hawk," Ben said grandly. "Plenty of room."

Ben took the bandages off his patient the next day. Though Hawk had been warned, he was still startled by what he saw. It looked as if a sledgehammer had smashed Cy's face out of shape. The eyeless socket was especially harrowing. But after Ben fashioned a patch to cover it out of a piece of leather, Cy's appearance improved somewhat. The damage to his jaw made it difficult for him to speak, but he was able to talk after a while, the words coming slowly, painfully, in a faint. rasping tone. By nightfall he was doing much better, however, and the next morning Hawk, leaning back against the cabin's door frame, watched him bid Ben good-bye.

"I told him to steer clear of any more Mandans," Ben remarked as he waved to Cy. "It's my thinking he will."

"I'll be moving on myself, Ben."

"No need to rush off. You look like you could use a rest."

"I'd only be bringing those bastards down on you, Ben."

"You think they're that close behind you?"

"I'm not sure. But it sure as hell won't do me any good to stay in one place too long."

"Don't be in such a hurry to ride out. I got fresh plews that need stretching and drying and I'd appreciate some help. Besides, I got a surprise for you."

"Oh?"

"I got myself a Crow squaw. She's off to visit her sister's village. Prettiest Crow you ever laid eyes on. When night comes, she sure as hell keeps me hopping." He chuckled and shook his head. "I'll have to admit it, Hawk. I didn't try to stop her from going. I needed the chance to recuperate."

"When do you expect her back?"

"Today, maybe. Tomorrow for sure."

"As soon as she gets back, I'll move on, Ben."

"That's right decent of you. But stay until then."

"Fair enough."

* * *

Two days later the Crow woman returned, riding a pretty spotted pony. Hawk's breath caught in his throat as she neared the cabin. It was Raven Eyes. When she saw him standing in the cabin doorway, she was as careful as he to show no emotion at all. To Hawk she was even lovelier than he remembered. Her slim, willowy figure filled out her beaded buckskin dress, and her braided tresses hung clear to her waist. She glanced boldly at Hawk as she dismounted and walked toward the cabin. Ben left the doorway and hurried to greet her, welcoming her back in the Crow tongue, his gravelly voice surprisingly gentle.

It was too late in the day for Hawk to ride out as he had promised, so he allowed Ben to convince him to stay one more night. Understanding Hawk's reluctance to be in the same room when a man and his woman made love, Ben had Raven Eyes fix Hawk a bed of straw and blankets in the barn's grain room.

A little past midnight, Raven Eyes came to Hawk, striding into the grain room and peering boldly down at him. He hadn't been able to sleep, and the moment he heard her footsteps entering the barn, he sat up. There was no window in the storeroom and in the near pitch-black darkness all he could make out at first was Raven Eyes' slim figure and the penumbra of black hair flowing past her shoulders. She went down on one knee beside him and only then did he see for sure that she was naked.

"What are you doing here, Raven Eyes?" he asked in Crow.

"You are a fool if you don't know," she replied.

"You have a husband now."

"He is no husband if he cannot satisfy his woman. I give him plenty time, but when I come back, he is still not a man."

"You ought to give him more time."

"What is the matter with me? Does he not want me? Why don't I make him hard?"

She leaned closer to him, her perfumed breath and the scent of her fully aroused body almost more than Hawk could bear. How was it, he asked himself, that Ben Bluebelly could not rise to the occasion for such a woman?

"Many times I think of that time I was with you," Raven Eyes told Hawk softly. "Ben says you are Golden Hawk. My father think this too, but he is not so sure. Is what Ben say, true? Are you Golden Hawk?"

Hawk nodded and saw the pride leap into her eyes. It was something to boast of, he realized, sleeping with the famed Golden Hawk.

"You are not an old man, Hawk," she assured him with a smile. "That I remember. Do you remember how it was with us?"

"It's not likely any man would forget you, Raven Eyes."

"That is what I think, too."

Her swift, eager fingers pulled off his long johns. She pressed her silken body close against his, her knees easing over his thigh and pressing into his crotch. He could feel himself swelling and swore softly.

This shouldn't be happening. Ben was his host. This was not the way to thank a man for his hospitality.

She grasped his erection, testing its rock-hard solidity. "You see?" she said eagerly. "I make you hard. Like before at Fort Hall. I can tell you want me. Is this not so?"

"Yes," he told her with a sudden, harsh eagerness, "I want you."

Laughing softly, she closed her mouth over his, her tongue snaking past his lips. His arms came up, he pulled her on his bed, then rolled over onto her, no longer thinking of Ben or hospitality or anything else—only how fast and how deep he could get into her.

She spread her thighs and he plunged in, feeling her warmth engulf his erection. Like a great she-cougar in heat, she flung her arms tightly around his neck and erupted under him, her nails scouring a path down his naked back. Once or twice her wild gyrations almost pulled her free of him, but she wrapped her powerful legs around his waist as she had before and locked her ankles behind his back.

Reaching bottom with each stroke, Hawk pounded on to glory until the dam burst and she began to gasp, then cry out, her fingers clutching convulsively at him as she too climaxed, her fingers grabbing his hair frantically. He thought she was trying to scalp him without a knife. But by that time he didn't care what damage she did to him.

He was coming again.

Afterward, Raven Eyes kissed him eagerly, sucking on his tongue like a harlot, her face covered with tiny beads of perspiration.

"Now it is my turn," she told him eagerly.

Before Hawk could protest, she was on top of

him, sucking his sagging manhood into her, then wriggling her buttocks to get his growing erection still deeper into her. Once that was accomplished, she grinned proudly down at him, her white teeth gleaming in the darkness. He found himself smiling back up at her, enjoying himself hugely as he reached up to cup her generous breasts in his big hands.

She was riding him frantically now, her head thrown back, her neck taut. Relaxing, he let her have her way with him, and soon they were nearing their climaxes. Coming before she did, Raven Eyes did not slow one whit, and when at last he fired up into her, it set her off all over again until she collapsed forward onto his chest.

Her deep sigh of contentment filled the tiny room. Then she kissed him. It was a long kiss, her tongue probing deeply, her hot breath mingling with his. Pulling her lips from his, she began to grind her pubis into his crotch. It didn't take long for him to be ready again—more than ready. Eager. She opened wide. He plunged into her. She pumped back frantically, just managing to hold back the moment of her climax for a few last thrusts of ecstasy. Exploding when he did, she managed to muffle her scream by pressing her mouth into the hollow of his collarbone.

She continued to pump, a reflex kind of action, unable to bring herself to halt what filled her with such pleasure. From her tiny cries, Hawk realized she was enjoying the aftermath of their lovemaking almost as much as what had come before. Finally her movements tapered off and she lay quietly beneath him while he remained in position on top of her, his flaccid manhood resting within her.

For a long, delicious while they remained in each other's arms, their labored breathing gradually quieting. Then, thinking it was all over, he started to pull out. But her hands tightened about his arms, clutching at him desperately, pleading for it not to end. So he let himself remain within the warmth of her while she lay still under him for a while longer, unmoving, holding him in place. Then he became aware of her hips moving, a slow lifting, then a half-turn. She kept it up, his head swimming with the pleasure of it. Abruptly, she tightened convulsively around his shaft, and he felt himself growing rapidly within her. The feel of him expanding inside her caused her to utter a tiny cry as she flung her arms around his shoulders and continued her maddening hip movement.

Though their lovemaking started slower this time, it ended with her feverish pumping, both of them pounding at each other in wild, sheer abandon until at last, completely spent, they lay quietly in each other's arms, panting. They could have kept it up all night, Hawk realized—and he was perfectly willing to try. But she had to get back to her master's bed, and soon.

The sound of Ben's heavy boots alerted them. With a soft cry of dismay, Raven Eyes rolled off Hawk as Ben pushed open the door.

"I know you're in there, Raven Eyes," Ben said, peering into the room's windowless darkness. "Get your Crow ass out of there and back to the cabin."

Without a word Raven Eyes got up and slipped past Ben.

"This is damned embarrassing, Hawk," Ben said, his voice tight with anger.

"Sorry, Ben," Hawk said, sitting up. "Didn't mean no harm. I knew her from the fort. She just sort of insisted."

"I guess any bitch has a right to be comforted when she's in heat. But that don't make me feel no better about it."

"These things happen, Ben."

"Hawk, are you still refusing to share the gold?"

"Ben, I don't have any gold."

"That's your last word, is it?"

"Yes, Goddammit, it is."

"Have it your way, then."

"What are you going to do to Raven Eyes?"

"I should have had better sense. Crow squaws are an adulterous lot, no better than whores. I'll let her pa keep the presents I brung, but I'm sending her back first thing in the morning."

Without another word, Ben swung around and left.

Hawk thought about it for a while, then shrugged and lay back down. After his recent exertions, he had no difficulty falling asleep.

Raven Eyes was gone before Hawk entered Ben's cabin the next morning. A surprisingly amiable Ben Bluebelly insisted that Hawk forget the previous night's unpleasantness and stay on a while longer. To assure Ben that he held no ill will, Hawk consented to stay with him one more day.

Early the next afternoon, Hawk thought he glimpsed riders on the canyon rim. Shading his eyes, he peered up but saw nothing. The sky was bright, the sun blinding. He could have been mistaken.

Later, Ben brought out his horses and saddled up.

"I let those mules drift too far," Ben told Hawk. "Guess I'll have to go after them. You're welcome to come along."

"I'll saddle my horse," Hawk said. "You go on ahead. I'll catch up with you."

A half-hour later as the two riders clattered over a caprock and rounded a sharp bend in the canyon, Ben Bluebelly pulled up suddenly and turned to face Hawk. There was a revolver in his right hand, its yawning muzzle aimed at Hawk's head.

"Now, just sit steady, Hawk," Ben told him.

"What the hell is this?"

Ben smiled bleakly. "Those riders you saw should be reaching this spot soon."

The click of iron on metal caused Hawk to look down the canyon. Cy was riding toward them and behind him rode three Comanche warriors, rifles held across the necks of their little patch-colored ponies.

Hawk looked back at Ben. "I never thought I'd see this, Ben—you throwing in with Comanches."

"Before you showed up, they came by looking for you. You can imagine how happy I was when you came by. As soon as I could, I sent Cy after them."

"But why?"

"The gold, you fool."

"You won't get any gold this way."

"We'll see about that. These Comanches promised that if I helped track you, they'd make you tell me where you hid that gold."

"You really believe they will?"

"Why not? I'm delivering you to them, ain't I?

And when they go to work on you, you'll be real anxious to tell me where that gold is. Afterward, I'll let them kill you outright. It'll be a real kindness."

Cy and the three Comanches were much closer now. Hawk knew he had to act fast. He had let Ben hang himself with his own testimony and felt no anger, only a weary sadness, as he reached back to the knife resting in its sheath at the nape of his neck.

Ben saw the movement and fired. But his horse moved slightly under him and his shot went wild. Hawk's knife went straight to its mark, the blade sinking deep into Ben's throat. The man sagged forward in his saddle, dropping his revolver as he grabbed his throat.

Spurring his mount past Ben, Hawk snatched the knife out of his throat, then shoved the gurgling trapper off his horse. Sheathing the knife, Hawk pulled his horse around and started to ride back up the canyon when he saw that the Comanches had him encircled. For a single instant Hawk considered bulling his way through them, but one of the Comanches spurred suddenly toward him and ran a lance into his side. Hawk toppled from his saddle.

The lance's wound was superficial, but when he landed on the caprock, he was momentarily dazed. Before he could get to his feet, two of the Comanches leapt from their ponies and hauled him upright. The third Comanche stepped toward him. He had a scar above his eyebrow and another that ran down his face to his chin. Hawk read nothing in his face but contempt—that and an implacable hatred.

Pushing his face close to Hawk, the Comanche chief spat a mouthful of phlegm at Hawk's face.

Then he smiled. "So this is the famous Golden Hawk," the chief said. "Why do you not fly away from us, Golden Hawk, like the Great Cannibal Owl?"

"You have dishonored Buffalo Hump's promise."

"Buffalo Hump is dead. Now the Kwahadi are free to go after Golden Hawk. Our band must be avenged for the killing of Two Horns."

"That was a long time ago."

"The Comanche do not forget such a betrayal." The chief smiled. "We will be famous when we bring you back to our village."

"Your village is a long way from here."

"So we start now, Golden Hawk."

Still on his horse, Cy had been watching them nervously. When the Comanche chief turned to stare at him, Cy glanced over at the writhing figure of Ben Bluebelly and then back to the three Comanches. Employing a crude sign language, he indicated he wanted to take Ben to his cabin. The two other Comanches promptly hauled the dying man onto his feet and flung him over the neck of Cy's horse and let loose with a series of chilling war cries, then slapped Cy's horse on its rear end. Cy tried desperately to remain in the saddle as the terrified horse bolted up the canyon. Long before horse and rider were out of sight, Ben's body had been thrown clear.

Hawk's wrists were quickly bound with strips of rawhide. A Comanche dropped a noose over his head and tightened it with cruel suddenness. Hawk gagged painfully and reached up with his bound hands to loosen the rawhide. Again the reata was yanked sharply, this time sending Hawk sprawling forward onto his face.

The Comanches mounted up. The one holding the reata wound it about his saddle horn, then kicked his pony to a quick canter, the others following. Stumbling awkwardly, Hawk kept on his feet for a few desperate yards until, unable to skirt a boulder in his path, he went flying and was dragged on his stomach over the canyon's rocky floor.

The Comanche dragging him pulled up, shouted to his fellows to watch, then yanked the reata, demanding Hawk get up. Wearily, painfully, Hawk raised himself onto his feet and braced himself. The other two Comanches reined in to watch. The Comanche yanked on the reata again, viciously. Hawk kept his balance and in cold, defiant fury yanked back on the reata as hard as he could.

He almost dragged the Comanche off his pony.

His two companions hurled derisive shouts at the Comanche.

The Comanche turned about in his saddle and urged his horse to a steady walk, jerking Hawk along every now and then, but never quite hard enough to cause Hawk to lose his footing. Grinning, the other two Comanches pulled up behind Hawk. The war chief was leading Hawk's horse and had appropriated his rifle, the Hawken that had once belonged to his father.

Hawk squared his shoulders and kept on, bitterly aware that it was a lust for gold that had caused a white man he thought was his friend to betray him to his Comanche enemies.

— 7 —

Joe Red Feather watched in grim satisfaction. This Golden Hawk was not invincible, after all. Barely able to keep up with the Comanche pulling him along, he was continually pitching forward to the ground, allowing himself to be dragged for long, grueling stretches before struggling back up onto his feet.

Not until nightfall did the Comanches make camp. Watching from a ridge, Joe Red Feather decided it was a good time for him to return to his own camp and see to the Crow woman he had taken the day before. He found her waiting for him, still unhappy and glowering, her hands securely bound behind her. He dragged her upright and flung her against a tree, then bound her to it with strips of rawhide. As he tied the last knot, she tried to kick him in the groin. He stepped back and casually slapped her about the head and shoulders until blood ran from her nostrils.

Then he left her and slipped silently back down through the timber. When he came within sight of their camp, he saw how well the Comanches entertained their captor. Their torments were ingenious. Watching Golden Hawk take his punishment filled Joe Red Feather with a deep, savage excitement. Soon he would be doing the same to Golden Hawk—all the way back to Blackfoot country.

Exhausted finally, the Comanches prepared their beds and Joe Red Feather moved back up through the timber.

As soon as he overtook the three Comanches the first time, he had doubled back to the captain and told him the Comanches were heading, not south, but due west, and were close behind Golden Hawk. The captain had accepted this lie without question and promptly headed west.

Slipping away from the captain at his first opportunity, Joe Red Feather had moved south again and had overtaken the Comanches. With them was a grotesque-looking trapper riding a paint. He was leading the Comanches down into a canyon. Not long after that, Joe Red Feather had witnessed the Comanche's capture of Golden Hawk.

It was then that he had come upon the Crow woman crouched on the canyon rim. She had an ancient rifle in her hand and was getting ready to fire down upon the Comanches holding Golden Hawk. He wrested the rifle from her and demanded to know what she was doing. She hated Comanches, she told him defiantly. Though he did not trust her, he let her believe he accepted this explanation. In time he would learn what the real reason had been for such foolishness.

* * *

He reached his camp, untied the Crow Woman, and took her repeatedly until she lay beneath him too exhausted and too filled with loathing to respond. But the hatred that flashed out of her impenetrable black eyes gave him no concern. She was a Crow. All Crow women were adulterous and had no shame. He would use her as he would any whore.

Tying her securely to the tree again, he reclined on his bed of fresh pine boughs and looked up at the glowing moon. At dawn tomorrow he would take Golden Hawk from his captors.

He slept, contented.

The Comanche's campfire sent a fitful glow over their campsite. This far from Comanche territory the three warriors had been careful not to disturb the silence of the timbered slopes with a victory dance. And they were careful to let no more than a few tendrils of blue smoke escape skyward.

But they had allowed themselves a small reward for their success in taking the fearsome Golden Hawk. Jabbing him with freshly sharpened sticks, they had waited until he was bleeding from countless wounds before they began kicking him about. At the end of it, they concentrated on his side and crotch. Yet even as they worked him over, they were profoundly uneasy, so famous and feared a warrior was Golden Hawk.

The Indians had bound Hawk sitting upright, his back against a tree, his wrists tied behind him. Asleep in front of him was Sore Foot Horse, the war party's chief. Weasel Tail and Comes Late slept on the other side of the fire.

But Hawk did not sleep.

Since the moment they bound him to the tree, he had been working to free himself. Forcing the rawhide to cut deep into his flesh, he had been using the fresh blood to help ease the rawhide over his fists. Only now was it beginning to work. But the progress was miserably slow. Meanwhile, the pain in his blood-slick, straining wrists was excruciating.

Abruptly, his thumb slipped out from under the bloody rawhide. A painful moment later, his entire hand was loose. A few seconds more and both hands were free of the rawhide. As the blood flowed back into them, Hawk suffered a painful bout of pins and needles. He rubbed his hands together behind his back until the discomfort faded and the circulation was restored. Working his arms free was the next problem, but it was accomplished within a few minutes and he stepped away from the tree, the rawhide on the ground before him.

Stepping out of its bloody loops, he studied the Comanches asleep before him. He had a score to settle with each one, and if he did not kill them at this moment, he would have to contend with them as long as they lived.

But to kill all three he would have to be quick. Very quick.

In the chill darkness before dawn, Raven Eyes watched Joe Red Feather come awake and fling aside his blanket. Rising to his feet, he groped through the timber in search of a spot to relieve himself.

"Free me," Raven Eyes demanded when he returned.

He untied her. She found a place in the timber and squatted. Returning to the camp, she approached him warily. "Will you keep me tied up forever, white man?"

He glared at her and replied in the Crow tongue, "I am not a white man. The blood of Blackfoot warriors runs in this warrior's veins."

"There is not much Blackfoot blood, I think," she remarked. "You stink too much of the white man."

He slapped her. She flung herself on him, her fingers groping for his throat. He managed to pull her hands away and fling her to the ground. When he began to kick her, she grabbed his ankle and twisted. With a startled cry, he pitched forward onto the ground. She spat on him.

"You bitch," he hissed as she scrambled to her feet. "When I return, I will deal with you."

"Deal with me now, if you can. Kill me! How else can you deal with a woman?"

"Whore, you mean!"

By this time she had worked herself around to his bed of pine boughs—and the rifle beside it. Snatching it up, she danced swiftly out of his reach and aimed it at him. Slowly he moved toward her, a sly smile on his face. At once she realized, he had no fear of her, or of the rifle she held. One swift glance down at the rifle told Raven Eyes why Joe Red Feather was smiling. The rifle had no firing caps.

"I would not kill you," she said, flinging the rifle at him.

He caught the rifle, astonished. "Why would you not kill me?"

She shrugged. "Maybe you tell the truth. Maybe

there is Blackfoot blood in your veins. There is some in mine too. Before I could walk, I was taken from the Blackfoot by a Crow raiding party."

"Which band?"

"I do not know. My Crow parents would not tell me."

"This rifle was not loaded. You would not have killed me even if you pulled the trigger. But I am pleased you did not pull the trigger. Maybe you and I should fight no more."

"But I am only a whore to you."

He shrugged. "I have a big mouth, I think."

"Where do you go now?"

His eyes gleamed as he told her. "Now I take Golden Hawk from the Comanches."

"Why do this?"

"I will bring him to my mother's people. Then I will be famous and lead their warriors in many battles. You come too, back to your own people."

"As your woman?"

He nodded quickly, eagerly almost.

"I will go with you, then."

As she followed Joe Red Feather down the slope, she recounted the many lies she had just uttered and smiled grimly to herself. This half-breed had used her like a whore and then he had called her one. Her heart shriveled as she recalled how he had taken her. He was such a fool, he would believe anything. There was no Blackfoot blood in her veins, only Crow and she would live to see his dream of capturing Golden Hawk come to nothing. But she would bide her time until the right moment.

It gave her great pleasure to contemplate what she would do then.

* * *

Hawk stepped away from the tree and walked lightly over to Sore Foot Horse's sleeping form. The Comanche's hatchet was within easy reach of his right hand, its blade sunk into an exposed root. Reaching down, Hawk worked the hatchet loose, then lifted the blade slowly past the sleeping warrior's face. Once erect, Hawk concentrated his gaze on the man's neck. He would have to cut through the jugular with enough speed to prevent an outcry.

At the first light of dawn, he struck.

The blade cut deep enough, severing the jugular, but not until Sore Foot Horse managed a sharp, brief whimper. At once the other two were on their feet. Hawk had no choice. He flung himself headlong across the fire at the two Comanches, driving the nearest one, Comes Late, violently back. As the Comanche staggered back, Hawk slashed at him with the hatchet, managing to slice deep into his shoulder. Blood spurting from the wound, the Comanche clasped his shoulder and staggered back.

But the third Comanche was now out of Hawk's reach and was calmly sighting his rifle at Hawk. Before he could squeeze the trigger, however, a hatchet flew out of the timber behind him, its blade slicing deep into the small of his back. The Comanche sagged forward, the rifle dropping from his nerveless fingers.

Startled at his unexpected deliverance, Hawk turned to see Joe Red Feather striding out of the timber, a rifle in his hand, a grim smile on his face. Seeing him, Comes Late, the Comanche Hawk had sliced in the shoulder, bolted for the timber. Joe Red Feather flung up his rifle, tracked the fleeing

Comanche briefly, and fired. The round whined off a tree. Comes Late vanished into the timber.

Behind Joe Red Feather, Raven Eyes stepped into view. Hawk found this almost as difficult to believe as the fact that Joe Red Feather had just saved his life.

"I guess I owe you, Joe," Hawk said.

"Looks like it, doesn't it?"

"Where the hell did you come from?"

"Been following these Comanches for some time now. The captain's been counting on them to track you."

Joe Red Feather leaned his rifle against a tree and with obvious satisfaction inspected the two dead Comanches. Then he took out his revolver and leveled it at Hawk.

"Just stay quiet now, Hawk," he said. "Real quiet. I'm taking you up north to Blackfoot country. There's plenty of braves up there who'll be glad to roast the soles of your feet."

"I thought you'd be taking me to the captain."

"To hell with that bastard. All he can think of is gold. He's a fool and he's crazy."

"And what are you?"

Joe Red Feather smiled. "Smart enough to catch you, and careful enough to keep you."

Turning to Raven Eyes, he told her to tie Hawk up, using the rawhide he had spotted at the foot of the tree, the same tree to which Hawk had been bound for most of the night. Raven Eyes picked up the rawhide and approached Hawk, Joe Red Feather covering Hawk with his revolver.

"What are you doing with this man?" Hawk whispered to her.

"I have no luck. He captured me."

"There's a knife at the nape of my neck. Give it to me."

"He has his revolver trained on you."

"I don't care. I would rather die here than at the hands of the Blackfoot."

Reaching up through Hawk's long hair, she fumbled for the knife.

"What the hell are you doing?" the half-breed demanded.

Desperately, awkwardly, Raven Eyes pulled Hawk's throwing knife from its sheath and gave it to him. As Joe Red Feather fired, Raven Eyes stepped in front of Hawk, taking the round in her left side. Hawk flung his knife. At the same instant, Joe Red Feather fired again. This time Joe Red Feather's bullet went over Hawk's head while Hawk's throwing knife lodged deep in his right shoulder. The breed dropped his revolver and staggered back.

But the blade was in a spot that could only incapacitate, not kill. Hawk flung himself at Joe Red Feather, driving him backward to the ground. Pulling his knife out of the breed's shoulder, he plunged it repeatedly into his chest. With each stroke, Joe Red Feather cried out.

Hawk kept plunging until Joe cried out no longer.

— 8 —

Hawk wiped his blade off on Joe Red Feather's britches, then glanced back at Raven Eyes. She was trying to sit up, one hand clasping her side, her face taut with pain.

Sheathing his knife, Hawk went down on one knee beside her to inspect her wound. The bullet had entered her left side just above her hipbone and come out a few inches behind it. Blood oozed from the exit wound in a slow, steady stream. Hawk ripped one of the dead Comanche's shirt off, ripped it into strips, and wound them around her waist as tightly as he could to stop the bleeding.

He retrieved his Hawken from the Comanche war chief and Raven Eyes insisted he return up the slope to Joe Red Feather's camp to get her flintlock rifle. That accomplished, he found his horse picketed along with those of the Comanches. Raven Eyes had a wealth of fine Comanche ponies to choose from, and when she had done so, he helped her mount up.

They rode on down the timbered slope, leaving

the dead bodies scattered behind them on the carpet of pine needles. Thinking back on it, Hawk felt a bit uncomfortable, especially at the rage that had consumed him when he pounced on Joe Red Feather. On further reflection, however, he chided himself for this weakness. He had done what had to be done.

With his pack horses and gear still at Ben Bluebelly's cabin and Raven Eyes needing shelter while her wound healed, Hawk headed back to Ben's cabin, arriving there late the next afternoon. It appeared deserted as they rode up the canyon toward it, then they pulled up warily a good hundred feet from it. If Cy were still in there, Hawk had no idea what kind of greeting he would get from him. The smell of wood smoke hung faintly in the air, but no smoke was lifting from the chimney. He looked around. No livestock were in the corral back of the barn, but coming from inside it, Hawk heard the restless stamping of a horse.

"Cy," Hawk cried, riding closer to the cabin, "you in there?"

There was no response. The silence was so profound Hawk could hear a door hinge creaking in the wind.

"I'm coming in, Cy," Hawk called. "I got a wounded woman with me. I don't want any trouble."

A crow flapped off the barn's roof, calling back in some annoyance. Hawk dismounted, lifted Raven Eyes gently down, and carried her up to the cabin. Kicking the door open, he stepped inside and let her down on an unmade cot in the tiny bedroom.

He glanced about him and saw signs of recent

occupancy everywhere he looked. The cabin's interior was a shambles. Whoever had been squatting in it was a futile and disorganized housekeeper. He went out to take care of the horses. Leading them into the barn, he saw why the horse inside had been stamping so unhappily. Its water bucket was bone-dry and every last bit of grain had been licked from its grain bucket. Hawk's two pack horses were gone, along with the gear he had stored in the barn. He figured that after Ben's death, Cy must have stayed in Ben's cabin for a night before taking the pack horses and gear and lighting out.

After unsaddling their mounts, Hawk grained the horses, filled two wooden buckets of water from the stream, and returned to the cabin. Raven Eyes was piling fresh wood into the dead fireplace.

"Get back on that cot," he told her. "I'll make the fire."

"It is not a man's work."

"You need your strength. Once you get it back, I'll let you make all the fires and lug all the water you want."

He saw her start to protest. Before she could, however, he put down his buckets and strode quickly over to her, swept her up in his arms, and carried her back into the tiny bedroom and again placed her down onto the bed. He was not gentle enough, it seemed. She cried out softly, then bit her lip for revealing her pain to him.

He leaned over her, concerned. "Does it hurt that much?"

She nodded.

"Let me take a look."

She kept her jaws clamped shut as he wound off the bandages. Both the entrance and exit wounds were festering. Angry red rims circled the holes and the blood that oozed from both of them was almost black. The wounds looked much worse than they had that morning.

There was no way he could avoid it. He would have to wash out the wounds thoroughly with strong soap if he could find any in the cabin, then cauterize them with his knife.

Three days later, Raven Eyes called him into the bedroom and pulled him down onto the bed beside her. Leaning over, he kissed her on the forehead and was startled at how warm she was. The day before there had been no sign of a fever.

"I have been sleeping too much," she told him. "I have bad dreams."

"I am sorry."

"I think I have not been very kind these past days."

"It does not matter."

"I forgive you. You hurt me, but I bleed no longer."

"The pain, is it still there?"

"It lives inside me like a small animal with sharp teeth."

He winced at the thought.

"Hawk," she whispered. "Take me back to my village."

"When you get well."

"No, tomorrow."

"How far is it?"

"Three, four days."

"Too far. We better wait until you shake this fever."

"Do as I say, Hawk. Please."

He hesitated for only a moment longer. "All right," he said at length. "I'll build a travois and wrap you warmly. We will leave tomorrow as soon as we can."

He held her in his arms for a long moment, then kissed her cheeks and then her forehead. She sighed, snuggled deeper into his arms, and fell asleep. He pulled gently out of her embrace and stood looking down at her. He was profoundly troubled.

She was sleeping so deeply, he thought. Too deeply.

They were leaving the canyon, following a wide stream. Ahead of them opened a long, undulating swale. A shot rang out. It came from the other side of the stream. Hawk pulled Raven Eyes' horse—travois and all—into a patch of willow and scrub pine, just as another rifle shot sounded.

Hawk flung himself off his horse. "Are you all right?" he asked Raven Eyes.

She nodded. "Poor Golden Hawk. Now who is it that must kill him?"

"I don't know," he said as he unhitched the travois and unstrapped her.

"Give me my rifle," she told him.

After digging it out of the travois load, he handed it to her. "I'll be back as soon as I can."

But he did not mount up again. He was suddenly very reluctant to leave her. Despite the way the travois had been bumping over the ground, she had been unable to keep awake.

She saw the hesitation in his eyes. "Go after this man," she told him, "or I will never see my village again!"

He stepped into his saddle, flung his horse about, and galloped out of the pines. Keeping his head low, he rode across the stream, heading in the direction from which the two shots had come—a clump of cottonwoods. Reaching it, he found fresh footprints in the soft ground. From their depth and distance apart, he knew the rider was pushing his mount hard as he fled back up toward the canyon.

He followed the tracks until he was once more enclosed by the vaulting walls of the canyon, his eyes on the rim above him. Almost too late he caught the flash of sunlight on a rifle barrel ahead of him. The report came just as he flung himself forward over his horse's neck and spurred the mount to a sudden gallop. The bullet whined off the rocks behind him. A second shot sent a round buzzing past his shoulder. Hawk spurred his horse on and kept going until the canyon wall hid him from the rifleman perched on the canyon rim.

Dismounting, he checked the Hawken's load and followed a game trail that took him swiftly to the canyon's rim and started back along it. Skirting boulders and leaping lightly over dead falls, his ears alert for any sound, Hawk trotted steadily along. Reaching a ledge flanked by pine, he slowed and, approaching with great caution, peered through the trees. Beyond the ledge was a grassy sward that gave a clear and unobstructed view of the canyon floor below.

It was from that spot, Hawk was certain, that the bushwhacker had fired upon him.

Through the pines Hawk stole, dropped behind a boulder, then moved around it and walked out onto the clearing. Reaching the edge of it, he saw the imprint of a prone form and two indentations where the rifleman's elbows had dug in while he aimed. He peered down at the canyon and saw nothing. Moving still closer to the edge, he lay flat and looked back along the canyon rim. Again nothing. A bristlecone pine was perched on the lip of the canyon, its gnarled roots reaching down the rock wall. As Hawk peered over at it, a rock wren—startled by his presence—flew out over the canyon, scolding as it went.

At the same moment he heard running boots close behind him.

Jumping to his feet, he whirled. Cy Martin was so close Hawk had no chance to bring up his rifle. Wielding his own rifle like a club, Cy caught Hawk chest-high and slammed him backward. Hawk dropped his rifle and tried to keep his balance as Cy clubbed him again and again, driving him back relentlessly. Cy had the strength and purpose of a maddened bull, but Hawk managed to grab the rifle's stock and yank it out of Cy's grasp.

Bracing himself to drive Cy back, Hawk felt the ground under his feet give way. He toppled backward into space. Something hard and unyielding struck him in the back. Reaching out, he grabbed hold of one of the bristlecone's roots and hung on. He had struck a ledge about ten feet beneath the rim.

Cy's mad, broken face appeared above him. He was infuriated to see Hawk staring back up at him.

He had obviously expected to see Hawk's body spread-eagled far below him on the canyon floor.

"What the hell's the matter with you, Cy?" Hawk demanded. "What're you after me for?"

"Ben saved my life—and you killed him!"

"He sold me out to the Comanches. You did, too."

"Ben told me all about you. You have a fortune in gold, but refuse to share it."

"Ben was mistaken."

"I don't care about that gold now. Or your lies." He aimed his revolver down at him. "You killed Ben, so I'm going to kill you."

As Cy fired, Hawk ducked aside, unholstering his own revolver. Cy's round ricocheted off the rock wall. A small explosion of rock shards dug cruelly into Hawk's face as he blinked and fired up at Cy. His bullet caught Cy high on his right shoulder, knocking him back, a heavy stream of blood pouring down his chest. Hawk heard pounding boots as Cy turned and fled. Hawk climbed up the bristlecone's roots and boosted himself up onto the canyon rim.

Hawk's rifle remained where Cy had dropped it. Examining Cy's rifle, Hawk found that Cy had split its barrel. Evidently, in his haste to fire on Hawk he had rammed too much powder into it.

Cy's heavy boot prints were not difficult to follow, and soon Hawk noted the dark bloodstains in the sand that accompanied his tracks. The wound did not seem to slow him down any, and not long after, Hawk lost Cy's tracks in some rocks, but kept going until he found a trail leading down into a tortured wasteland of gullies and washes.

The dark entrance to a narrow canyon beckoned

to him across a flat—a good place to lick your wounds. Hawk made for it. Halfway across the flat, he saw the dim imprint of Cy's boots. The man was still loosing blood, but he was striding right along. Moving faster, Hawk kept low. A few feet from the canyon, a shot from within it exploded dirt at his feet.

Darting to one side, Hawk kept going until he was out of sight of the canyon entrance. Then, hugging the rocks, he doubled back to the canyon. Within a few feet of it, Cy shouted out to him.

"I can hear you coming, Hawk. Hold on! I'm a wounded man. I'll throw out my weapon and come peaceably."

"Do it then."

An instant later, Cy's revolver hurtled through the air and landed a few feet in front of the canyon entrance. Hawk waited for Cy to emerge. When he didn't, Hawk crouched lower and called, "Come on out of there, Cy. If you don't, I'll come in after you."

"Hold on, can't you?"

"Why should I?"

"I told you. I'm wounded! I'm not fit to shoot it out with you. I'm finished."

It was clear Cy was stalling. Hawk entered the canyon. A few yards into it, he was nearing the face of a great boulder when a sudden explosion of hooves came from behind it. Hawk looked up as a horse pounded around the boulder and bore down on him. Cy's head was down as he lashed the horse with his squirt. Hawk tried to jump back out of the horse's path. He was too late. The horse's flaring nostrils and bulging eye brushed his face, and then the animal's massive chest sent him hurtling back to the canyon floor.

Hawk could only manage a single shot at Cy as the man rode from the canyon. Running out after him, Hawk saw Cy looking back, his single crazed eye bulging wide with fury. That one glimpse was all Hawk got as Cy galloped down a sudden slope and disappeared, the sound of pounding hooves fading rapidly.

— 9 —

Raven Eyes was slumped back against a tree, her eyes closed, her rifle in the grass beside her. For a moment Hawk was afraid she was dead, but as he flung himself from his horse and ran to her side, she opened her eyes and smiled wanly.

"Did you get the one who shot at you?"

"I wounded him, but he got away."

"Do you know him?"

"Cyrus Martin."

"The one Ben took care of?"

"Yes."

"No wonder he missed with his long rifle. He has only one eye. But why does he shoot at you?"

"For killing Ben."

"Ah! I remember that. Ben gave you to the Comanches, so you killed him with your throwing knife. You are very brave. I tried to help you then, but Joe Red Feather prevent me."

"You helped me later. You saved my life."

"Now you are saving mine. You are taking me to

my people. I think I will be better when I feel the pines."

Heading toward a dim cluster of foothills an hour later, Hawk glanced back at Raven Eyes. Bundled snugly on the jouncing travois, she was sound asleep. He turned back around in his saddle and hoped that was a good sign.

He was riding up a gentle rise when the Crow warriors materialized on the crest just ahead of him. Hawk pulled up. The Crows regarded him solemnly and made no outcry. Among them was Black Horse wearing a magnificent war bonnet, his long, braided hair reaching past his stirrups. The others wore their hair in upswept pompadours stiffened with clay. Beads dangled from their necks and they wore bracelets. The dandies of the Rockies some called them, and it was an apt description.

Black Horse recognized Hawk at once and booted his pony down the slope toward him. Hawk dismounted to greet him. Raven Eyes remained fast asleep on the travois.

"Why does Golden Hawk ride into these hills?"

"I am bringing back Raven Eyes, Black Horse. She has been wounded."

As he spoke, Hawk indicated with a quick glance the travois behind him. A corner of the blanket he had wrapped around Raven Eyes had fallen over her face, so that Raven Eyes was not visible from where the two men were standing. Almost pushing Hawk out of his way, Black Horse hurried around to the travois and flipped back the blanket.

For a moment he studied Raven Eyes intently, a deep concern etched on his face. Then he stepped back and fixed Hawk with a harsh, angry gaze. "Who has done this to her?"

"Joe Red Feather."

"I know him. I will seek him out. He must die."

"That's already been tended to, Black Horse."

"You killed him?"

"Yes." Hawk looked back down at Raven Eyes. "She asked me to take her to her own people. She has no place left to go. The bullet went through her left side. But now she has fever."

Black Horse looked at Raven Eyes. "She is close to death."

"How far is your village?"

"Not far. I will send word to prepare my lodge."

Black Horse called out to one of the Crow warriors waiting on the ridge. The Indian peeled his pony back and vanished. Hawk placed his hand on Raven Eyes' forehead. Though he had been stopping constantly to give her water, her forehead was almost searing to the touch.

Hawk mounted up, as did Black Horse.

"Follow me," Black Horse told him.

In less than a quarter of an hour they broke out into a lush, pine-studded park. The village consisted of a cluster of close to thirty tepees set up in the grassy bend of a mountain stream. Birch and alder stands flanked the stream. The air was clear and sweet with the scent of pine. Hawk understood at once why Raven Eyes had been so anxious to return here.

Black Horse led Hawk toward a large tepee set up on a slight knoll quite close to the stream, a judicious distance from the rest of the encampment. Hawk followed. Once he dismounted in front of Black Horse's lodge, he was shunted aside by Morning Star, Raven Eyes' sister, and the other women of Black Horse's lodge. Swiftly they unstrapped her from the travois and carried her inside the tepee.

Hawk followed in after Black Horse and crouched down to watch as the women lowered Raven Eyes gently down onto the bed of fresh pine boughs they had already prepared for her. Over the pine boughs had been placed a thick buffalo rug. Abruptly the band's medicine man burst into the tepee, his gourds rattling, his feet jingling with each pounding, dancelike step he took.

Hawk glanced at Black Horse. "Who is this one?"

"Crooked Leg. He is our band's medicine man."

Like Hawk, Black Horse showed little enthusiasm for the medicine man's sudden appearance.

Except for the slight bend in his left leg, Crooked Leg was a fairly handsome Indian. He was wailing now, his head flung back, his eyes rolling into his head. The women gave way before him as he began dancing about Raven Eyes, scattering from a small pouch what appeared to be ashes. Soon, his wailing cries became an anguished screech that rose and fell constantly, nearly shattering Hawk's eardrums. After a while of this, Crooked Leg produced a tiny brass bowl in which something was burning. Whatever it was, it caused a sickening stench. Before anyone could stop him, Crooked Leg placed the brass bowl down on Raven Eyes' chest. The stench aroused her—as it did everyone in the tepee—and Raven Eyes began to twist her head from side to side, moaning.

That was enough for Golden Hawk. He got to his feet.

"This is not my lodge," he told the medicine man sharply, "but you must leave, Crooked Leg."

Crooked Leg whirled to face Hawk, his eyes flashing defiantly in his darkly handsome face. "My medicine will save the chief's daughter."

"It will make her sick. Get out."

"But who will care for her?"

"The women of this lodge will tend her."

Furious, Crooked Leg flung up a rattle and shook it in front of Hawk's face. Hawk stepped toward him and ripped the gourd from Crooked Leg's grasp, flung it down, and stomped on it repeatedly, grinding it into the hard-packed ground.

Aghast, the women in the tepee drew back. Even Black Horse seemed alarmed.

From his medicine bag, Crooked Leg took something and held it out before Hawk. It was a dead, mummified field mouse. Waving the tiny dead animal in front of Hawk's face, Crooked Leg advanced. Hawk waited calmly, then snatched the dry, shriveled little body from the medicine man's hands and flipped it back into his face. Then he grabbed Crooked Leg by the shoulder, spun him around, and boosted him toward the tepee's entrance. Hastily flinging open the flap, Crooked Leg scrambled out, Hawk following.

Outside the tepee Hawk positioned himself between Crooked Leg and the tepee's entrance. Crooked Leg crouched furiously before Hawk. For a moment Hawk thought the medicine man was going to thrust another rattle under Hawk's chin. If so, Crooked Leg thought better of it. Instead, he sent a withering string of curses at Hawk, punctuating each one with an ominous shake of his rattle. Satisfied that he had done all he could for the moment, he flung himself about and stalked off.

Hawk reentered the tepee. Someone had flung away the brass bowl, and Morning Star was feeding her sister a dark, thick broth. At the same time the other women were dipping doeskin compresses into buckets of water, then laying them carefully down upon Raven Eyes' forehead, neck, and arms. Soon they had peeled nearly all of her clothes off and were busy placing more cooling compresses over her entire body.

Raven Eyes was fully awake by this time and seemed to be taking in eagerly the nourishment her sister was feeding her. As Hawk made himself comfortable, he glanced over at Black Horse. What passed for a smile lightened the old warrior's face, revealing his approval of how Hawk had handled the medicine man.

Early the next day, high in the pines above the village, Crooked Leg placed a blanket down in the middle of a small clearing. Then he sat down cross-legged on the blanket and proceeded to place upon it his most potent charms, after which he raised both arms to the sky, calling upon his totem, the fleet and clever red fox. He prayed long and earnestly, his voice rising and falling in a queer singsong that ended every now and then in a sharp, snapping bark.

For almost an hour he prayed in this fashion, after which he arranged his charms in a geometric shape on the blanket before him, then hauled out of his medicine bag the dusty, well-handled corpse of a bullfrog. Placing it carefully down in the center of his charms, he unsheathed his knife and plunged it through the bullfrog's back, leaving it impaled on the blanket.

His ritual completed, Crooked Leg relaxed. Golden Hawk no longer held any terrors for him. A sign would show Crooked Leg how to vanquish him. Until then he would remain inside his lodge, keeping vigil on his sacred rug, while he waited for the sign from his totem.

There was, after all, no sense in moving upon Golden Hawk before he was ready.

But the sign came almost at once.

As he was preparing to return to his village, Crooked Leg caught sight of a friendly red fox moving along a fallen log not twenty yards distant. As Crooked Leg watched, the fox paused to turn and glance at him, inviting him to follow. Then it leapt from the log and vanished into a wooded ravine.

Hastily, Crooked Leg mounted his pony and cantered after it, following the ravine until it emptied out onto a long, grassy flat. He did not see the fox, nor did he expect to, but he saw something else, a thin pillar of smoke drifting up from a campfire in the valley beyond the flat.

Urging his pony on across the flat, the medicine man angled down the valley's gently sloping flanks until he came out onto a ridge above the campsite. Squatting before the fire was a white man. He was alone, his back to Crooked Leg. At once Crooked Leg understood the fox's intent. This lone white man's scalp and entrails were to be used by Crooked Leg to concoct a curse on Golden Hawk.

Dismounting, Crooked Leg tied his pony to a sapling, took out his long butcher knife, and stole down the slope, moving through the tall grass as silently and stealthily as his totem, the friendly fox.

Cyrus Martin was chilled clean through and his thoughts were as bitter as wormwood as he contemplated his luck so far in attempting to get Golden Hawk for killing Ben. He supposed he was lucky to be alive. Hawk came close to killing him when he fired up at him from that ledge. Yet, Cy Martin had not given up.

His shoulder wound was damn painful, but would heal soon enough. Because he had no rifle, he had kept his distance while trailing Hawk from the canyon. Twice he had stolen close enough to risk a shot from his revolver. But he was too well aware by this time of Hawk's incredible luck, and dared not chance it. His revolver was not functioning properly, and one shot at a time was all he could manage with it.

Specifically, the trouble was that after a shot, the cylinder would not rotate, forcing him to turn the cylinder manually. He had just finished loading it. Now, frowning intently, he eased back the hammer to examine the cylinder more closely, hoping to see what the trouble was.

A sound came from behind him—that of a foot pressing on dry grass. He spun about. A crazed Crow Indian was rushing him, his knife held high. One look at the revolver in Cy's hand filled the Indian's face with dismay. Thrusting out his revolver, Cy squeezed the trigger, drilling a neat black hole in the center of the Crow's forehead. The Indian's knees buckled. Cy stepped aside as the

Crow stumbled past him and collapsed, facedown, into Cy's campfire.

Stupefied, Cy looked down at the smoldering body. The thought occurred to him that maybe some of Golden Hawk's luck had rubbed off on him.

The next morning—his stiffening corpse slung over his pony—Crooked Leg returned to his village.

The sensational news spread swiftly. As soon as Black Horse heard it, he sought out Golden Hawk. He was on the stream's bank, washing his socks and buckskin shirt. Side by side on the bank, his boots stood while he splashed about in the shallow water.

"Join me, Black Horse," Hawk said, standing up. "The water's fine."

"We will walk among the pines instead."

Unaware of Crooked Leg's arrival, Hawk was feeling immensely relieved—even content. He had just come from visiting Raven Eyes and was convinced that though she was still very weak, she was getting better. The warmth in her eyes as she gazed on him was still with him.

After laying his socks and buckskin shirt out on the grass to dry, Hawk pulled on his boots and moved off with the chief. In the pines above the village, they found a flat boulder and made themselves comfortable. The chief took out his clay pipe. Hawk did likewise. His tobacco was favored by the chief and Hawk gladly shared it with him. After both got their pipes going, the chief took a few troubled puffs and leaned back.

"Crooked Leg is dead," he said.

"What killed him?"

"A bullet through the brain. The one who killed

him sent him into the village on Crooked Leg's own pony."

Hawk had not seen the medicine man since their disagreement in the chief's lodge. He had supposed Crooked Leg had gone off to sulk, and was finding it difficult to feel any remorse.

But he was careful not to say or even imply this. "Did he have any people to mourn him?"

"His mother. She ran off into the woods to grieve alone. Already she has done much to herself. This will surely hasten her death. Crooked Leg was her only provider."

"It is a sad day for the village."

Black Horse nodded sagely. "Many talk now of your treatment of him. Many are certain you killed him."

"I did not kill him, Chief."

"I know that. Golden Hawk did not need to kill him. I did not like him. He was an evil presence in our village. His medicine cured no one. He could only make matters worse. With him gone, the village is a better place."

"But you think I should move on."

"Yes, Golden Hawk. There is already much fear of you in the village. At the council I have been questioned sharply at your continued presence. Many fear you will bring the Blackfoot down upon us. It is known throughout these hills how the Blackfoot seek you."

"The Crow hate the Blackfoot even as I do."

"That is true. And this would make you a brother to the Crow. But there are Crows who would like the honor of taking your scalp. And there are those Crows who have suffered at your hands. Many bands have sent chiefs to our councils to remind our people of this."

Hawk understood. Black Horse had nothing against him personally, but at the moment it would be best for all concerned if he pulled out. He was no longer welcome in the village—or in the Crow nation.

Hawk shrugged fatalistically. "I understand, Chief. My heart grows heavy at this news. Golden Hawk likes this village and its people."

"I do not want to see you go. But you must. And soon, Golden Hawk."

"I will leave before this sun sets."

Black Horse was relieved. "That is best for all concerned."

Hawk had heard of a wagon train pushing west through the mountains not far from here. A few Crow braves had already visited it to trade for sugar and salt. The settlers had been friendly and had done nothing to anger or insult the Indians. Perhaps these settlers could use a scout familiar with this country, one who might wish to join them in their westward trek to new lands.

Hawk had worn out his welcome in this one.

— 10 —

When Hawk entered Black Horse's tepee, Morning Star got up and moved away from Raven Eyes. Hawk could tell that Morning Star knew he was leaving. He knelt beside Raven Eyes, bent, and kissed her on the cheek.

Her eyes fluttered open and she turned her head slightly to look up at him. Her face was still gaunt, her eyes sunk in hollows, but her once-pale cheeks now had some color in them.

"Morning Star has told me," she whispered. "Where will you go?"

"To the other side of the mountains," he told her.

"What is that place called?"

"Oregon."

"I have heard of it. Many settlers pass through our land to go there, but I do not want you to go."

"It will bring trouble to your people if I stay."

"Go, then. But I think you will return to these mountains someday."

He smiled. "You think so, do you?"

"You will return and again build your cabin."

He shook his head sadly. "I do not think so." Then he took her hand. "Tell me, Raven Eyes. I have often wondered—why did you not come here when Ben sent you away? If you had, Joe Red Feather would never have captured you."

"Ben was very angry that night. He told me how he would punish you. You are a greedy man, he said, and that is why he sent the one-eyed one after the Comanches."

"So you waited on that canyon rim with your flintlock."

She nodded.

He squeezed her hand. "You are a very brave woman. I will miss you."

Tears gleamed in her eyes. "Thank you for bringing me home to my people."

"It was the least I could do."

"Go now," she said. "Short good-byes are the best."

He kissed her on the lips, then hurried from the tepee, his heart aching. It seemed he was always coming upon those who were eager to kill him or saying good-bye to those he loved.

A day later, Hawk realized he was being followed. Earlier, he thought he had glimpsed a wolf in the timber keeping pace with him. Thinking it might be the same one he had mended back at his cabin, Hawk pulled up to peer more closely at the timbered slopes above him.

He saw no wolf. Instead, he caught the glint of sunlight on metal. He rode on for a half-mile or so, then dismounted, glancing quickly back. For a split second he saw the outline of a horse and rider against the horizon.

Hawk was not surprised. He had looked closely at the bullet hole in the medicine man's forehead. The bullet had come from a revolver, not a rifle. For some crazy reason a trapper or someone else in the vicinity had come upon Crooked Leg and shot him.

And there was a damn good chance the trapper was Cy Martin. Recovered from his wound, the son of a bitch had managed to track Hawk to the Crow village and was now trailing him, waiting for his chance. But if this were so, why had he not tried to bushwack Hawk before this? A perfect time would have been while he was taking Raven Eyes back to her sister's village. Even as he asked the question, he knew the answer.

Cy Martin still had no rifle.

Which explained why it was a revolver he had used to kill Crooked Leg.

If the Crows who had advised him of the wagon train's direction had spoken the truth, Hawk would overtake it before nightfall. Lifting his horse to a lope, he reached the pass they had mentioned well before sundown, and kept on until he caught sight of the wagon train. Turning his horse, he rode up into the timber clothing the nearest mountain flank, his head down to clear the branches. After a couple of hundred yards, he dismounted and tethered his horse.

He moved swiftly back down the slope until he could see open ground beyond the timber. Peering down through the trees, he waited for the rider trailing him to appear. He was little more than a dark form against the bright pass beyond when at last he came into view. The rider halted and appeared to be considering whether or not to continue into the pass and overtake the wagon train. Suddenly he turned his horse and followed Hawk's tracks up the slope into the timber.

Hawk recognized Cy Martin's ravaged face. The mount he was riding was one of Hawk's pack horses.

Cy was able to follow Hawk's tracks into the timber for only a short distance, the pine needles obliterating any further tracks. Nevertheless, Cy kept going in the direction the hoof marks indicated.

Hawk grabbed a branch and hauled himself into a pine. They grew so close at this level that once Hawk had reached a height of twenty or so feet, he found himself able to clamber from tree to tree. Opening the loop of his reata, Hawk crouched on a solid branch and waited for Cy to pass under him. Before Cy reached Hawk's tree, however, he held up, then changed direction slightly. Hawk crossed to a tree farther up the slope and moved out onto another branch. This time Cy did not pause, but rode on directly under Hawk.

Hawk let the noose fall. As lightly as a snake, it dropped over Cy's head. Cy snatched at the rawhide to lift it off his shoulder, but Hawk yanked the loop shut, then ran back along the branch, dragging Cy off his horse. Looping the reata around a branch, Hawk dropped to the ground and hauled on the reata, hauling the dazed Cy up onto his feet. Then he wound the rope around a tree trunk, unsheathed his bowie, and approached Cy, who lifted frantically onto his tiptoes to keep the reata from tightening about his neck.

"Hello, Cy," Hawk said softly.

Cy's tongue flicked out to moisten his bone-dry lips. He could barely manage a scratchy moan.

"You'll be dancing on air in a few minutes," Hawk told him.

The man struggled feebly to stay on his toes, both hands grasping the rawhide. "Please . . ." he managed.

"But maybe there's been enough killing, Cy."

Hawk saw a desperate hope spring into the man's eye.

"I can see why you want to avenge Ben's death," Hawk assured him. "Hell, that's to be expected, considering how he took care of you. You owe him that much, at least."

Cold sweat covered Cy's forehead. Stepping closer, Hawk pressed the point of his knife against Cy's throat.

"Now, listen closely, Cy," Hawk continued with gentle reasonableness. "I could send this knife into your gullet, and then there would be one more death to mark my trail."

Cy's single eye opened wide in terror—and supplication.

"Promise to leave me alone, Cy, and I'll cut you down. There's only one condition: if I ever lay eyes on you again, you'll hang. Is that clear?"

Cy nodded quickly, then gagged painfully as this movement caused the rawhide to dig deeper into his windpipe. Hawk let the man struggle for a moment, then pulled him close and yanked the noose over Cy's head. Gasping, both hands up to his throat, Cy sank to the ground.

"Is it a deal, Cy?"

"Yes," Cy gasped painfully. There was no gratitude in his eye, only sheer terror.

"Good. And I think I'll take back my pack horse. I'll leave your saddle and possibles behind."

Holding his throat, Cy made no protest.

Hawk picked up Cy's revolver and emptied the bullets into his palm. "You killed that Crow back there, didn't you?" he said, tossing the empty revolver at Cy's feet.

"Yes," Cy admitted, his voice trembling.

There was no need for further conversation.

A moment later, his retrieved pack horse trailing him, Hawk left the timber. As soon as he vanished from sight, Cy scrambled to his feet and raced down the slope after him. Emerging from the timber, he saw Hawk riding hard to overtake the wagon train.

A sudden rush of wind caused Cy to glance skyward. Dark clouds were piling in over the foothills, sweeping close to the ground in spots, like smoke from a fire. A sharp edge of cold wind struck him, and a second later the rain began to pelt down in hard, driving drops. Cy shrank back into the protection of the timber.

The next morning the rain was still coming down. The wagon train had camped before a friendly little mountain stream that had turned into a wildcat overnight. Hawk had been welcomed by Don Turnbolt, the wagon master, and together they stood on the riverbank along with a few of the settlers, gazing on the turbid, steadily rising water.

"We should have crossed yesterday," said Turnbolt, "no matter how late it was."

Hawk nodded. They had not done so because the women had demanded they make camp on this side. It had been late, they had been wet, and the children had been getting impossible to handle.

So the decision had been made to cross early the next morning.

"We'll just have to wait," Turnbolt said, "until this rain lets up and this here river turns back into a stream."

"It'll give us a chance to repair some wagons," said one of the settlers.

"If we can keep dry enough," the man standing beside him said, staring gloomily at the surging waters.

Turnbolt glanced at Hawk. "You said you'd help out by shooting us fresh game as well as scouting for us. We're all getting pretty sick of salt pork. Now's your chance to put that fine Hawken to use, Jed."

Hawk had introduced himself by his Christian name, Jed Thompson. "Sure thing. You want to come along?"

Turnbolt grinned broadly. "You're damn right I do."

Of course, now that they were on the hunt, all game vanished. For the rest of that day and most of the next, the two men slipped noiselessly through the drenching woodland. When at last they pulled up on the edge of a clearing a little after noon, Hawk found himself thinking of a dry canvas-covered wagon back at the encampment—and of Jenny Winslow, the widow driving it. She had been doing a fine job of keeping him warm of late.

"Maybe we'd do better keeping in one place," suggested Hawk, gazing out over the placid meadow. The lush grass was almost blue in the wet light. "We can't do any worse than we've been doing."

"And it's a helluva lot easier," Turnbolt responded.

A man close to fifty, Turnbolt had admitted to Hawk that his only experience for leading this wagon train to Oregon was a book on the Oregon Territory he had picked up in a Salem, Massachusetts, bookstore extolling the virtues of the new land west of the Rockies. Tall, rawboned, with a granitelike lantern jaw and dark, piercing eyes, he was the kind of man that easily inspired others, and Hawk had no difficulty understanding how he had been able to lead so many innocents this far. But Turnbolt had been eagerly grateful when Hawk showed up, and he had not hesitated to admit to Hawk how much he needed his help in leading his people the rest of the way.

For close to fifteen minutes the two stood silently in the gentle rain, waiting. Then Turnbolt took off his big, wide-brimmed, black hat and swept it down to get the moisture off its brim.

Slapping it back onto his head, he looked gloomily at Hawk. "I suggest we give this up as a bad job. I'm so wet, I'm liable to take root right here and sprout branches."

"Stay a while longer," Hawk cautioned. "We've been here less than a half-hour. That ain't long."

Without a word, Turnbolt wearily shifted his weight to his other foot.

"Quiet," Hawk whispered urgently. "And don't move!"

A large buck—a ten-pointer at least—had suddenly appeared in front of them. Like an apparition, the deer had materialized suddenly out of the shifting curtains of rain obscuring the far side of the meadow. It was a blacktail, larger than a mule deer, with glowing, yellowish red on its breast and belly.

Keeping as silent and as immobile as statues, the two men watched the buck's steady approach, its antlered head moving quickly from side to side in its search for possible predators. Still well out of rifle range, the buck halted and looked back to the edge of the clearing from which he had just emerged. At once a doe and a yearling stepped out of the timber, glided swiftly into the meadow, and proceeded to browse.

It was then the buck's turn to feed. The moment his head ducked to the sward, both men raised their rifles and stepped forward. They moved steadily closer to the buck until a whisk of his tail alerted them. They froze. The deer's head shot up, and the animal looked directly at them for a long moment. It had seen both men without a doubt, but since they hadn't moved a muscle, the buck regarded them as nothing more dangerous than a tree or a queer stand of brush.

The buck resumed browsing. Hawk and Turnbolt edged closer to the feeding animal, being infinitely careful to keep themselves ready to halt instantly. Twice more the deer was alerted, and each time the buck gazed straight at the two frozen riflemen for a moment or so, then looked swiftly about and continued his feeding.

Within range at last, Turnbolt aimed carefully and fired. His bullet powdered one of the buck's antlers. Beside him, Hawk fired at the already moving animal and brought it down.

Turnbolt glanced with admiration at Hawk. "That's sure some rifle," he said. "I knew when I saw it that it was a genuine Hawken. You say it belonged to your daddy?"

"Yes," Hawk replied.

"Well, he'd sure be proud of that shot you just made."

Without replying, Hawk hastened toward the downed buck. It was big enough to give them each a load as they trudged back to the wagons.

A good three hours later, as the two men stepped out of the pines beside the last wagon with the fresh deer meat slung over their shoulders, a fortuitous rift in the clouds overhead allowed a golden shaft of sunlight to bathe them and the rest of the encampment in its heartening glow.

It was an omen.

Soon the rain would cease entirely, everyone agreed as they crowded about the successful hunters. The next day they would be across the river and on their way again.

Hawk did nothing to discourage their optimism and, dropping his burden allowed Jenny Winslow to lead him away. His buckskin pants were sopping wet by the time they reached her wagon.

"You must get out of those wet things at once," she said. "Get into the wagon."

Without protest, he clambered up into her wagon. She entered after him and closed the rear canvas opening. There was enough light coming in through the canvas for her to see his hesitation.

"What's the matter?" she asked softly. "Take off those wet things. I have dry buckskins for you."

"What else do you have for me?"

"Don't you know?"

"We better wait till later."

"If I wait another day—another hour—I think I will explode. Do you understand me?"

In case there was a likelihood that he didn't understand, she yanked off her skirt and flung her blouse over her head. As he had suspected, she wore no corset or chemise. The nipples on her full, melonlike breasts came erect and seemed to reach out for him.

He peeled out of his pants, underpants, and shirt and took her in his arms, his lips closing about her cherry-red nipples. It was good, so goddamned good, to feel her warm, undulating flesh under him, her breath on his ears as she leaned back to let him enter. When he did, she cried out softly in eager, happy anticipation.

Time telescoped. In the dim interior of the wagon everything happened swiftly, without pause, as if they were lost in a different world, another time. Wrapped in a fiercely passionate embrace, rocking and moaning, they climaxed almost heedlessly, and then they dozed as if they had become intoxicated by the potency of their lovemaking.

Jenny awakened first and without a word forked her strong legs over his waist. He became erect upon awakening. With a delighted laugh she plunged down upon his erection, took both his hands in hers, and leaned back. Their hands remained entwined as she rode him. Without willing it or thinking about it, he climaxed, as did she. He caught her as she collapsed forward onto his chest, panting and crying out softly like a wounded cat, her long auburn hair in her face, her chest rising and falling steadily from her exertions.

"My," she said at last, "that was nice. So very nice."

Beside her, his long limbs resting against hers, he traced a circle around one of her nipples, then took it lightly between his forefinger and thumb and played with it lightly. "Yes. It was good."

"I am worried that the settlers will find out about us and think I am a harlot for sleeping with you."

"I don't think so. They will understand."

"Perhaps. But do you understand?"

"What do you mean?"

"We are not married. We are not even engaged. Yet we have just made love. Doesn't that make me immoral?"

"Perhaps in some men's eyes, but not in mine."

He leaned his face close to her breast and closed his lips around the nipple he had been fondling. She placed her hand on the back of his head and pressed him gently into the lovely warmth of her breast. His lips worked gently, his tongue flicking lightly at the nipple's tip.

"Is that your answer?" she gasped softly.

"Yes."

She sighed and drew his face deeper into the warmth of her breasts and Hawk knew she no longer gave a damn what anyone else thought—and neither did he.

— 11 —

The skies were clear by morning. Two days later the raging torrent had gone back to being a fordable river. But when Hawk saw the wagons lining up to move across it, he did not like what he saw. He was not the wagon master, however. Turnbolt was—and under his leadership the wagon train must have crossed many rivers before this one.

Nevertheless, Hawk watched with growing apprehension as the lead wagon approached the riverbank. It was driven by Deacon Whittington and his wife, and after a nod from Turnbolt, who was at the river's edge astride his horse, they calmly urged their four-horse team toward the bank. It was as if they were out on a Sunday drive and were about to cross nothing deeper that a puddle in the road.

Galvanized by this sight, Hawk galloped down the line of wagons and cut in front of the deacon's wagon before it reached the water.

"You better hold up, Deacon," Hawk told him.

"What are you up to, Jed?" Turnbolt demanded, riding up alongside Hawk. "We've crossed rivers before. We know what we're doing."

"You don't know mountain river, Turnbolt. This one especially. Do you have any idea what the bottom of this one is like right now—after that torrent finished passing over it?"

Turnbolt pulled his horse back and looked out at the river. It was still running fast and there was enough silt in the water to prevent him or anyone else from glimpsing the bottom. Or knowing how deep the bottom was at that point.

"You're right, Jed," Turnbolt said soberly. "This sure don't resemble them placid streams we crossed on the flats below. What do you suggest?"

Hawk dismounted and walked over to the river's edge. Turnbolt joined him there and Hawk explained the problem. After a period of flooding, the normal fording places in a river often shift or become clogged with loose sand deposited by the powerful undercurrents. Someone was needed to cross on foot to find the exact location and condition of the ford, then mark it for the wagons. Only then should the wagons start across.

"You take charge, then," said Turnbolt. "The men'll do what you say if I give the word."

"Agreed," said Hawk.

Joshua Beechwood, a tall black-bearded settler, volunteered to wade across the stream and seek out the ford's location. As he waded across—the water up to his neck in places—he planted long saplings into the sand wherever the bottom was sufficiently solid. When he had reached the other side, he had marked the ford's placement and everyone could see for themselves how sharply it now slanted downstream. But this was a happy circumstance, Hawk pointed out, since now the wagons would not be trying to buck head-on the stream's still quite rapid flow.

Hawk sent two settlers across the stream to shore up the opposite bank with fresh earth. Once that was completed, the horses were watered thoroughly to make sure they would not pause to drink upon entering the stream. If they did that, the wagons would swiftly bog down.

The deacon's wagon was driven across by Turnbolt himself. Another settler—Bob Curry—walked in front of the horses, guiding and pulling them along with a rope, while Beechwood rode on horseback on the downstream side of the wagon, his whip ready if needed to keep the team moving as fast as possible.

In like fashion, each wagon that followed was driven across by Hawk and safely parked on the other side. When it was time for Jenny's wagon, Hawk climbed up beside her and winked. Wearing a bottle-green dress, she looked especially fine this morning, her cheeks glowing, her hazel eyes alight with excitement.

"Looks like we've saved the best for last," he told her.

"Get us across, Jed, and I'll reward you properly."

Halfway across the stream the wagon's wheels sank deeper than any of the others had. What had been hard-packed sand was now giving way under the pressure of so many wheels digging across it. Hawk jumped up and shouted at the horses, Beechwood's whip snapped across their backs. Redoubling its efforts, the team, straining mightily, pulled the wagon through the loose sand and climbed the far bank.

Hawk's reward was immediately forthcoming.

Jenny took off Hawk's hat and kissed him while the settlers crowding about the wagon cheered.

Smollett looked at the pitiful wreck Digger had just dragged into their camp. His face was a mess and he had only one eye. It looked like he had been kicked in the face by a horse. Or maybe two horses. He was barely conscious and Digger let him drop to the ground.

"Who the hell have you got there?" Smollett asked.

"Cyrus Martin, he says."

"What's the foolish bastard doing down out here in the middle of nowhere?"

"He ain't told me yet, and I ain't asked. What'll we do with him?"

"He's your responsibility. You decide."

"Maybe I'll feed him. The poor son of a bitch might know where in the hell we are." Digger pulled the man to his feet and poked him toward the fire.

Watching them go, Smollett scratched a mosquito bite and took a drag on his pipe. He had found some sweet grass and was smoking that. He was out of tobacco and was trying anything that would burn—grass, tree bark, even reeds. So far he had found nothing that served as an adequate substitute for tobacco, and he was in danger of having a nicotine fit.

He took a long drag on the sweet grass.

As that no-account breed had instructed them, Smollett had gone due west after Hawk. But they had not picked up the trail of the three Comanches, let alone that of the man they were after. All Smollett and his weary searchers had found in their trek westward were trees and mountains, each one higher than the one before. But at least they were heading west. And if they kept on in that direction, they would come to the sea, and the captain had already discussed with his men the likelihood of commandeering another ship.

Smollett slapped his leg, then his thigh. Anything would be better than these hellish mosquitoes.

With Tim Prew clinging to his sleeve, Digger hurried over to Smollett. It was Digger who spoke. "Captain, that fellow we just brought in knows where we can find Hawk."

Smollett forgot all about mosquitoes. He took his pipe out of his mouth. "What's this?"

"We gave Martin some of that old rank meat we left out too long, and he tore into it like a famished wolf. Between bites he started whimpering about Golden Hawk."

"How well does he know him?"

Digger grinned wryly. "I'd say he knows him well enough. Hawk killed the man that saved his life."

"Sounds like the right man, all right."

"Then he bushwhacked Martin and stole his horse."

"And this fellow knows where we can find Hawk?"

"That's what he told me, Captain. He saw Hawk heading west, riding toward a wagon train not far from here."

Tim cried eagerly, "Let me get him, Captain."

"You?"

"If he's in one of them wagons, I'll slit his throat."

"I don't want his throat slit."

"But, Captain, he must have the gold with him."

Smollett peered intently at the old blind man. "What're you driving at?"

"Why, that's easy, Captain. Hawk wouldn't be lighting out for Oregon Territory empty-handed. He wouldn't leave all that gold behind!"

Smollett could not deny the logic of that. "Maybe you're right, Tim. But there's no need for you sneaking into any wagons at night. There's a better way for us to get our hands on Hawk—and the gold."

"How?" Digger asked.

"I'll tell you when the time comes. First things first. We got to find that wagon train." He smiled. "And we'll let this here Martin find it for us. Give our poor beat-up mate more coffee and this time give him fresh meat."

Digger left in such a hurry that Tim Prew almost fell down trying to hang on to him.

Hawk studied the itinerary Turnbolt handed him. He had bought it, he said, from a mountain man in Independence, Missouri. It read:

> Cedars on bluffs, Grass and wood all the way up the trail from river. Water in parkland rimmed with cottonwood. Good camp.
>
> Seven miles. Trail over ridge to meadow. Then parkland. Water and good grass. Deadman's Canyon end of parkland.

Hawk handed the itinerary back to Turnbolt, who folded it carefully and placed it in his Bible.

"We're going the right way, looks like," Hawk told the wagon master. "There's just over seven miles to the canyon. We should reach it easily by tomorrow afternoon. It'd be a good idea to keep on through it and camp on the other side."

"I agree," said Turnbolt, beaming. "I'll feel a whole lot better with that canyon behind us—and Oregon just ahead."

The next afternoon Hawk rode up alongside Turnbolt and pointed. Shading his eyes, Turnbolt saw what Hawk had already glimpsed. He grinned and slapped his thigh. A welcome gap in the line of snowcapped peaks was opening before them, Deadman's Canyon.

When they got to within a mile of it, Hawk saw a narrow, pine-covered ridge on the canyon's southern flank, and dropping almost straight down from it, a sheer wall of rock. The other side of the canyon was equally precipitous. The canyon appeared to have been chopped out of the mountain by the single strokes of a monstrous ax.

More than likely, Hawk realized, it was just another river.

Hawk looked back at the wagon train. The evenly spaced wagons filled the gently sloping parkland with dust as they rumbled and creaked toward the distant pass. Hawk's eyes swept to the south and caught sight of a herd of antelope moving off in long, soaring leaps.

He was about to look back when he caught sight of a lone horseman cresting a hill well beyond the antelope. It was an Indian. Something about the way he sat his horse caused Hawk to leave the wagon train and canter toward the Indian for some distance before pulling up to a halt and peering more closely at the horse and rider.

Comanche.

Hawk didn't know how he could be so certain at

this distance. But certain he was. This was more than likely the third Comanche, the one who had fled into the woods as Joe Red Feather fired on him. His name was Comes Late.

Hawk turned back to the wagon train. There was nothing he could do until the Comanche made his move. At least now he had a warning. He thought it best not to worry the others, Jenny especially.

Hawk did not doubt that Comes Late would come for him when he felt the time was propitious. He had already come this far. A Kwahadi Comanche did not turn back.

Before entering the canyon, Hawk halted the wagon train and scouted the canyon thoroughly. He saw no sign of the Comanche, but for the third time in as many days he glimpsed a wolf in the distance. Hawk rode back to the wagon train, waved it on, then waited for Jenny's wagon to pass him. He clambered up beside her and ducked into the wagon. He was saddle-sore and weary. Leaning his back against a rug piled against a bureau, he tried to get some rest.

The wagon train was almost through the pass when Hawk heard Jenny's gasp. She halted the wagon so quickly Hawk's head slammed back against the bureau. Poking his head out to ask Jenny the reason for halting, he saw what was hanging from the ridge above them.

It was a white man, his neck bent at a sharp, unnatural angle, twisting slowly in the wind.

Screams came from women up and down the wagon train.

"My God, Jed," Jenny said. "What does it mean?"

Hawk jumped down from the wagon and lifted

his already loaded rifle, intending to sever the rope with a bullet. Before he could fire, he heard a low, gut-deep rumble coming from behind them. It sounded like the canyon was shifting its weight. He glanced back. Two massive boulders were bounding down the steep wall, gathering enough debris and rock in front of them to be almost completely hidden by the growing, leaping shroud that clothed them as they reached the canyon floor. With tremendous, rolling bounds they thundered across the canyon and with a fearsome crunch smashed into the rock wall opposite, disintegrating into great, jagged chunks.

Only slowly did the dust begin to settle, revealing an uneven pile of debris stretching across the canyon—a wall of rock and dirt taller than any of the wagons. For a moment or two afterward, rivulets of loose sand poured down onto the canyon floor while small stones bounced down the face of the slope like afterthoughts.

Then came an awesome silence.

Hawk did not hesitate. He swiftly untied his mount from the rear of Jenny's wagon and raced forward along the wagon train. When he overtook Turnbolt and Beechwood, he found them gazing back at the avalanche in amazement, enormous relief showing on their faces that they had not been caught under its terrible, destructive force.

"Get the train moving," Hawk cried. "We'll be trapped in here."

"Trapped?" Turnbolt cried. "What are talking about? The avalanche missed us."

Without bothering to argue, Hawk galloped on past them until he reached the deacon's wagon.

The deacon was standing up on the wagon seat staring back at the dust still rolling up from the canyon floor, ignoring completely the body twisting in the wind over his head.

"Get going," Hawk told him.

The deacon turned and sat down on his seat. His distraught wife stared out at him from the wagon.

"What about that man up there?" she cried, pointing.

"Never mind that. Move out!"

The deacon gathered up the reins. But even as he did so, Hawk sagged back in his saddle. They were too late. Another deep rumbling filled the air. Ahead of them another avalanche swept down from the canyon wall and after a short, gut-wrenching rumble, swept across the narrow canyon, depositing a second wall of debris in their path.

The trap had been sprung.

Dismounting, Hawk snaked his rifle out of his saddle sling. He aimed carefully up at the rope holding the slowly twisting figure and squeezed off his shot. His aim was good. The rope frayed, then parted, and the body plunged heavily into the dust of the canyon floor. Mounting up again, Hawk rode out to examine the body. He dismounted, rolled the body over with his toe, and found himself gazing at Cyrus Martin's shattered visage. Behind Hawk came the pounding of hooves.

He turned as Turnbolt and Beechwood flung themselves from their mounts. "Jed, what's all this about?" Turnbolt asked.

"I'm not sure yet."

"Do you know this man?" Beechwood asked.

"Yes."

"My God! Who is he?"

"A trapper who got beat up pretty bad by some Mandans a while back. He's been after me."

"Why?"

"It's a long story, Josh."

Hawk gazed up at the canyon rims towering over him. There was no doubt in his mind now why the wagon train had been halted in this fashion. Only a large, well-organized band of men could have managed those twin avalanches.

Captain John Smollett and his crew.

"We'd better get back to the wagons," Hawk said. "Right now."

"What about this man?" Beechwood asked, indicating Cy Martin's sprawled figure.

"Leave him for the vultures."

Beechwood was shocked, but before he could protest, a rifle shot from the canyon rim caused the ground to explode at Hawk's feet. Another rifle shot rang out and the ground in front of Beechwood exploded also. Shaken, Beechwood rocked back, staring wildly up at the canyon rim.

Hawk leapt astride his mount, pulled his horse around, and galloped back to the wagons, the others following. The shots flung at them from the rim came close, but served only to give their horses wings. Reaching the wagons, Hawk told the settlers rushing to meet them to pull the wagons into a circle and fort up.

"Indians?" one of the women cried.

"No," said Hawk bitterly. "Pirates."

A moment later, Captain John Smollett and several of his crew rode toward them. Hawk recognized the riders flanking Smollett. Within a hundred yards of the wagons, Smollett pulled up, tied a white handkerchief to his rifle barrel, then continued on. Hawk heard a shout from Beechwood and Turnbolt and turned to see them coming toward him.

"Can't talk now," Hawk told them as he untied his horse from the rear of Jenny's wagon. "I got business with them gents out there."

"My God, Jed," protested Turnbolt. "What's this all about?"

"The gent waving the white flag is Captain John Smollett. That's some of his hellish crew with him."

"Pirates? Out here?"

"I don't have time for explanations now." Hawk swung into his saddle and rode out to meet the captain. About twenty yards from him, he reined in his mount.

The captain smiled broadly, the picture of affability. "We only want your gold, Mr. Hawk. Bring it out and I'll let the wagon train move on. I won't take no women to comfort my men and I won't allow any plunder of those wagons, neither."

The predatory look in his eyes told Hawk a different story. Gold alone would no longer be enough to satisfy this man and his cutthroat crew. "I don't believe you, Smollett."

The captain rocked back on his horse as if Hawk's words had offended him. "Why, mate, you've got me word. Soon as I get that gold, me and my men want nothing more—except fair winds at our back and sheets full to hurry us on our way."

The captain was still a windbag, Hawk told himself. But that didn't make him any less dangerous

"Why did you kill Cy Martin, Smollett?"

"Cy had served his purpose. He was the bloke directed me to you and this wagon train."

"And for that you killed him."

"I needed something dramatic—eye-catching, you might say—to stop this wagon train in its tracks. You must admit, it did the trick. Now, I want that gold. You got it stashed in one of them wagons, I presume."

"You presume wrong."

"Then where is it?"

"There is no gold, Smollett."

"This is getting tiresome, Hawk. Very tiresome."

"For me as well, Smollett."

Smollett glanced up at the sun, then back at Hawk. "You have until sundown. If by then you don't ride out here with that gold, our men will take the wagons and everything else of value."

Smollett lowered his rifle and pointed it at Hawk. The other riders did the same.

"You can go back to the wagons now," Smollett told Hawk.

Hawk pulled his mount around and started back.

Just before he reached the wagons, he heard the sudden thunder of hooves as Smollett and his men rode back the way they had come. He felt raw with frustration.

He and many innocent men, women, and children were caught in a corked bottle.

— 12 —

Hawk finished telling Turnbolt and the rest of the men what Smollett wanted, then leaned back against the wagon wheel to wait for their response.

It was not long in coming.

"I say we fight the bastards," cried Bob Curry.

Three, then four more men spoke up in agreement. Turnbolt and the deacon, however, did not appear as eager for battle.

Beechwood took his pipe out of his mouth and peered closely at Hawk. "You say you do not have that gold?"

"Not a single coin."

"Well, then." He shrugged and looked around at the others. "I guess that settles it."

"The thing is," Hawk pointed out, "gold's not all they're after. They want what you have in these wagons, and I wouldn't put it past them to take your women as well."

The deacon bristled, "You don't know that for sure, Jed," he protested. "You're just saying that to arouse us."

"I'm telling you what I think, Deacon."

"But you don't know for sure."

"No."

"Good," said the deacon, obviously relieved.

"Well," Bob Curry broke in, "I think it would be a damn good idea for us to listen to what Jed thinks. I say we stick with Jed and not give an inch to those bushwhackers."

Many of the men muttered agreement to that. But not all. There was a definite split in the settlers on this issue, and Hawk detected an eagerness in some of them to wash their hands of Hawk. These were the men who either did not believe him when he insisted he had no gold, or who didn't care one way or the other just so long as they were left out of it.

"Get back to your wagons, men," said Turnbolt. "Jed won't be bringing any gold out to them pirates, and that means we're going to have to beat off their attack, if they meant what they said."

Talking to one another in low, anxious tones, their faces revealing the fear they felt for their women and children, the men hurried back to their wagons to make preparations.

Hawk crossed the ground within the circle of wagons, pushed past one of Jenny's draft horses, and climbed up into her wagon. On the floor at the back and front of the wagon, Jenny had lined up the rifles and revolvers they had loaded earlier.

She was crouched in the far corner of the wagon, looking out at the sudden commotion. The frightened voices of the women carried into the wagon. "There's going to be trouble, Jed, isn't there?"

"More than likely."

"I do so hate violence."

"We all do."

"Then why, Jed? What do those men want of us?"

He leaned back next to her, took out his pipe, and lit it. Once he got it going to his satisfaction, he related to her the entire business starting with Pete Foxwell's visit to his cabin. When he had finished, she said nothing. He waited, then turned his head to look at her. She was staring at him.

"But, Jed! It's . . . so incredible."

"Yes."

"And I believe you don't have the gold."

He said nothing in response, wondering why she felt she had to assure him of that.

She looked out at the canyon. "Now, what?" she asked fearfully. "We just wait here for them to attack?"

"I don't see we have any choice. They have us bottled up pretty good. But we have a good defensive position. The captain's men will have to cross open space to attack the wagons. I don't figure they have that much sand in their craw. They'll more than likely try to starve us out, but we've got more food and water than they have."

"You mean we're under siege as well?"

"I'm sorry, Jenny. But that's the way it looks to me. The important thing is for us not to lose our heads."

"That's easy for a man like you to say."

"Now, what's that supposed to mean, Jenny?"

"You're one of those mountain men. You've lived with savages. You know all about fighting. This sort of thing is nothing for you."

"That's not true, Jenny." He put his arm around her to comfort her.

She rested her head on his shoulder and spoke to him in a soft, tiny voice. "I'm so frightened, Jed. I'm just not very brave. Not when it comes to this sort of thing."

"It's the waiting, Jenny. When Smollett makes his move, you'll feel better."

His words gave her little comfort. Jenny shuddered at the thought like a small animal caught in a trap.

How in hell, Hawk asked himself, could that blind man have found him? Only his head and shoulders were visible as he boosted himself silently into Jenny's wagon. Hawk lifted his revolver and fired.

The blind man cried out and tumbled backward. Leaping out of the wagon after him, Hawk saw the white-haired blind man scurrying frantically about like a terrified bug. He rammed into the rear of a wagon, rebounded, then slammed into one of Jenny's draft horses. The huge animal reared in terror, knocking the blind man to the ground, squealing. The horse came down hard, its hooves biting deeply into the blind man's side. For a moment he writhed on the ground like a stomped worm, then went quiet.

The shot had awakened the settlers. The men rushed through the darkness from all quarters. A lantern was lit, then another as someone peered down at the twisted figure on the ground.

"Put out those lanterns," Hawk cried.

Before they could, a sudden volley of rifle fire from just outside the ring of wagons extinguished both lanterns. The flaming coal oil splattered about, spreading fire over the ground and then up the wheel of a nearby wagon.

A second later the captain's men reached the wagons.

After almost fifteen minutes of hard, close-in fighting, the settlers beat off Smollett's forces and sent them fleeing back into the cover of darkness. But the damage inflicted by the attackers was considerable. One wagon had burned to the ground and two settlers had been wounded, one of them Bob Curry, who suffered a shoulder wound that left him in considerable pain.

Hawk killed a man he knew to be Digger. He had seemed crazed and was yelling something about the blind man as he came at Hawk. Three more of Smollett's men had been wounded, but had been able to pull out with the rest.

On Hawk's insistence, the settlers kept up a vigil until dawn, then tried to get some sleep, a few men keeping guard. They got little sleep. As soon as it was light enough, the captain's men opened up from the canyon rim, sending a deadly, frightening fire into the wagons throughout the day.

Not until dusk, when the firing ceased, did the men gather to discuss their situation. They met close to the canyon wall, where they would be reasonably safe from any random fire from above. As the men gathered, Hawk leaned back against the wall and kept his silence as Turnbolt opened the meeting.

"Well, men, we've beat them back," Turnbolt

pointed out. "That's something. And we stung 'em pretty good."

"Oh, sure, Turnbolt," said a settler in the rear. "Now it's a turkey shoot—and we're the turkeys."

"My wagon is riddled," another complained.

An old man in back, whose son had been wounded, snorted angrily, "They'll wipe us out. Mark my words! Our bones will bleach in this canyon. We'll never see Oregon."

"That's enough, Amos," said Turnbolt. "It isn't as bad as all that."

"Well, it soon will be," snapped another settler, fixing a malevolent gaze on Hawk.

"So what do you suggest?" Beechwood asked.

The settlers exchanged quick glances. One of them started to say something, but reconsidered and kept his silence. It was obvious that many of the settlers had discussed their options and had already decided what needed to be done, and Hawk had a pretty good idea what they were thinking. They wanted to throw him to the wolves.

"I'd like to say something," Hawk said, pushing away from the canyon wall.

"Go ahead, Jed," said Turnbolt.

The men turned to stare at him. Hawk saw few friendly faces. "I know I brought this on you," he admitted. "And for that I'm sorry. But it isn't only me the pirates want. It's the entire wagon train."

"You're right about one thing," snapped one of the settlers. "You brought them bastards down on us. And maybe it ain't just you they want. But we don't know that for sure. I think we ought to see if we can't deal with these fellers."

"A deal?" Hawk asked.

"Yes. Your hide in exchange for this wagon train."

"Wilson," Turnbolt cried, "that's uncalled for!"

There was an immediate uproar, everyone talking at once. It was impossible for Hawk to tell how many were in favor of dealing with Smollett and how many thought it was a lousy idea. But it didn't matter. The rabbit was out of the hat. Whether or not to deal with Smollett was what every settler had been considering.

"We can argue about this all day," cried another settler above the uproar. "I say we vote now!"

"You men make me sick," cried Turnbolt, his voice thick with contempt. "You can't trust that cutthroat out there. I'd sooner deal with the devil himself."

"Vote," someone cried.

"Let the women vote, too."

There was quick agreement to that. A settler hurried to get them. A moment later the women arrived, joining their husbands eagerly, their children underfoot.

Hawk saw Jenny and nodded a greeting to her. She returned his nod nervously and stayed with the woman she had arrived with.

"All right," said Turnbolt angrily. "Vote all you want, but count me out. I won't be a party to this."

He strode angrily through the crush of settlers to stand beside Hawk, his arms folded defiantly.

Beechwood stepped forward and cleared his throat. "All those in favor of dealing with the outlaw, raise your hand."

Half the men's and most of the women's hands shot up. Hawk kept his eyes on Jenny. Without the slightest hesitation, her hand went up with the majority.

"This isn't personal, Jed," Beechwood told him. "We have no choice in the matter. We must think of our women and children."

Turnbolt snapped angrily, "Cowards always need excuses for turning tail, Beechwood. But that doesn't mean anyone has to believe them."

"That's uncalled for," snapped the deacon.

A heated discussion followed to see who would contact Smollett. Hawk did not stay to hear it and left the settlers to pick up the gear he had left in Jenny's wagon. He had gathered up most of it when Jenny hurried up to him.

"Where are you going?" she asked.

"I'm pulling out."

"But you can't."

"Who's going to stop me?"

"Jed, they've appointed a committee to keep you here until Beechwood and the deacon can speak to the captain."

"Interesting."

"You must understand, Jed. We have to get to Oregon. All that matters is for us to get there. We've sold everything, pulled up stakes, left our families behind. You must see our side of it."

"The trouble is, Jenny, dealing with that cut-throat might damn well make it impossible for any of you to reach Oregon."

"Surely that's not true. These men are not savages."

Hawk saw it was useless to talk sense to her. Without saying good-bye, he walked off toward Turnbolt's wagon. Before he got there, four settlers, all carrying rifles, stopped him.

"Sorry, Jed," one of them said. "We have to keep you here, in case you're thinking of running off."

"Get out of my way."

One of the men began to drift around behind Hawk, a short length of rope in his hand.

"Take another step," Hawk told him, "and I'll shove that rope up your ass."

The fellow halted uncertainly. Then the other two men came at Hawk. Before Hawk could turn completely to face them, something hard and unyielding struck the top of his head. Hawk plunged to the canyon floor into a fathomless darkness.

Hawk regained consciousness in front of the grain wagon, his hands tied behind him, his ankles bound as well. He had been propped up with his back to a grain sack. His head rocked painfully from the blow he had received. Apart from that he was well enough.

Then he heard it again—the voice that had awakened him. It was Turnbolt. Hawk shook the cobwebs out of his head. "That you, Turnbolt?"

"You all right?"

"What the hell do you mean am I all right?"

A plank in the floor lifted and Turnbolt's head appeared. The wagon master pushed two more planks aside to allow room for his shoulders.

"Had to wait till you came around," Turnbolt explained softly as he boosted himself up into the wagon. "You been out for close to three hours."

"Has the deal been set with the captain?"

"You're to be delivered at dawn. Like a lamb to slaughter. The captain has assured Beechwood and the deacon that in payment for this craven betrayal, his men will help haul our wagons past that barrier."

"And the settlers believe him."

"They're too scared not to believe him."

"Poor bastards," Hawk said.

Moving up beside Hawk, Turnbolt slashed through the ropes binding him. "Leave here as quietly as you can. I fed the one they left here to guard you enough whiskey to put him to sleep for a week. Here's your bowie. I couldn't get hold of your rifle or your revolver."

"Damnit, Turnbolt," Hawk said, taking the knife. "You know what store I put by that rifle. It was my father's."

"Then stay here and look for it."

Hawk understood Turnbolt's exasperation. Hawk would have to leave the rifle, then. His revolver, too. "They'll climb all over you when they find me gone, Turnbolt. What are you going to do?"

"Leave that to me, Jed. Now get out of here while you can."

The two men shook hands and bid each other good luck. Hawk squeezed through the hole and slipped past the inebriated guard. Keeping close to the canyon wall, he kept going until the wagons were lost in the darkness behind him.

Pulling up, he rested back against the canyon wall. His pounding head made thinking straight nearly impossible. After a moment he stepped back from the canyon wall and peered up the nearly sheer wall of rock, searching for a way up to the canyon's rim. He did not find what he wanted until he was within a few yards of the barrier of boulders and rocks blocking the canyon. A series of ledges led to a game trail that disappeared into the night above him.

The trail he found of only marginal help. Clinging to the rock face as we worked his way up the wall, he was at times barely able to see his hand in front of his face. He kept going, nevertheless. Close to dawn he pulled himself up onto the rim and set out to find the captain's camp. He expected to find it close to the rim—and did, the glow of a dying campfire marking it for him in the distance.

Slowly, cautiously, he crept closer. The captain and all his men were asleep around the fire. It was the captain Hawk wanted, but which sleeping form was Smollett's? He crept so close he could hear the men's even breathing. Slipping among the sleeping forms like a great cat, he came at last upon the captain. He was closest to the fire, a heavy blanket over him. Lifting the edge of the blanket, Hawk saw the captain's rifle beside him. And a holstered revolver and gun belt.

He strapped the gun belt around his waist and moved the rifle out away from the sleeping form where he could reach it in a hurry. Then, before Smollett could cry out, Hawk's forearm crunched down on his windpipe.

"Listen and listen good, Captain," Hawk whispered, leaning close. "One sound from you and I'll crush your windpipe."

Smollett reached up to grab Hawk's forearm. Hawk leaned slightly forward. Smollett's eyes bulged out of their sockets and his attempt to free himself ceased.

"That's better," Hawk whispered softly. "Now get up and head for those pines over there."

As Smollett got to his feet, Hawk snatched up his rifle, dug the point of his bowie into the man's back, and urged him on. Meekly, the captain walked ahead of Hawk through the sleeping men. As they passed the last one, he stirred, muttering something in his sleep. Hawk pointed the rifle down at him and waited. When the man rolled over and pulled his blanket up over his shoulders, Hawk poked his blade into Smollett's back and they started up again.

"Where's your horses?" Hawk asked as soon as they were clear of the encampment.

"Over there." Smollett pointed to a low granite ridge outlined against the night sky.

When they reached the horses, Hawk pulled up beside a disorderly pile of saddles and rendered the captain unconscious with a single hard, slicing blow to the side of his neck. Picking out a horse, Hawk saddled it, draped the captain over its neck, and mounted up.

Keeping in timber, he rode steadily until he put the canyon well behind him. His hope in separating Smollett from his men was that without their leader, his crew might possibly give up the siege of the wagon train. That hope was dashed less than an hour later when Hawk heard far behind the dim rattle of gunfire and realized that the captain's men were just as greedy for plunder—and women—as Smollett was.

Hawk tried not to think of Jenny.

— 13 —

"There ain't nothing you can do about it," said Smollett. "Sooner or later you're going to have to give me that horse of yours and let me go. You can't stay awake forever."

The captain was facing Hawk with his back against a tree, his hands tied behind him, his ankles bound also. In the campfire's leaping flames, his eyes gleamed with arrogant confidence. And he was right. Hawk was exhausted. He had not slept for a day and two nights.

He got up and walked over to Smollett and inspected the rawhide binding him. It was still tight. Smollett was no threat, not for now, anyway.

"We'll talk about this some other time, Smollett."

Hawk found a spot some distance from the fire that gave him a clear view of the captain; he rolled into his blanket and, with his hand resting on the rifle he had taken from the captain, dropped off almost instantly. The chill of early morning awakened him. Smollett was standing over him, his retrieved rifle leveled at Hawk.

"I'm ready to talk now," Smollett told him, his smile cold.

Hawk sat up. Smollett's wrists were bloody. There were deep furrows where the rawhide had cut through the flesh. But this was not hampering his handling of the rifle.

"She's all primed," Smollett said. "I'm going to be taking your horse, Mr. Hawk."

"Take it, then."

"But first I'm going to blow your head clean off your shoulders."

"Don't you want me to take you to the gold?"

"This might surprise you, but I believe you now. You don't have any gold. You wouldn't be riding away from that wagon so easy if you had it."

"Then take the horse and go. Let this be an end to it."

Smollett smiled meanly. "That's what you'd like, wouldn't you? But I'm not about to let you off that easy. You've cost me considerable loss, Hawk. Mates I'll never see again are feeding the vultures because of you. Tim Prew is gone. Digger. And many others. They're never going to hear again the wind in the rigging or feel the hard slap of salt spray as they come on deck."

Afraid the captain would go on forever, Hawk said, "You're a windbag, Smollett. Shoot me and be done with it."

Smollett lifted the rifle and sighted along its barrel. "Bless me, but I guess I will."

A pale streak bounded out of the timber. Smollett saw the wolf he'd thought dead out of the corner of his eye and turned, emptying the rifle into the animal's chest. Though the wolf was fatally wounded this time, its impetus was enough to knock Smollett off his feet.

Hawk's throwing knife was in his hand instantaneously. As Smollett scrambled back up onto his feet, Hawk sent the knife into his chest. The blade sank deep into Smollett's heart. He sagged to the ground, a look of pure surprise on his face.

Hawk dropped to one knee beside the wolf's body stretched full out on the ground. The wolf's mouth was rigid in a silent snarl, its glazed eyes staring blindly ahead. A few of Hawk's stitches still hung from its belly. Since joining the wagon train, Hawk and others had occasionally glimpsed the wolf in the distance loping along parallel to the wagon train. If there had not been so many noisy, unreliable humans crowding close upon Hawk, the wolf would probably have made its presence known to him.

Hawk buried the wolf deep enough to prevent its bones from being dug up by coyotes, left Smollett to the buzzards, and rode on, aware of one final gauntlet—the Kwahadi Comanche he had spotted.

Until then, Hawk would just have to wait. He was still many nights and days from Fort Hall, and he doubted his luck would continue to hold. But it did not seem to matter. He could not shake a deep weariness of the soul. It seemed to him that a lust for gold had poisoned almost every person he knew. Aside from Turnbolt, the only one in all this wilderness who had not turned on him was that poor dumb brute that lay now under a thin mantle of earth.

It was the bright, splashing, cooling sound of the spring water that led Hawk to push through the timber to the pool. Dismounting, he filled his hat with water and satisfied his mount's thirst. Then he flung himself down on his belly like one more beast of the forest, scooped up the icy water into his cupped hands, and slaked his own thirst.

Feeling much better, he sat back against a tree. He was about to fumble for his pipe when a shadow fell over the pool. Hawk knew enough not to reach for anything. A moment later the Kwahadi strode into view and came to a halt in front of Hawk, his rifle resting easily in the crook of his left elbow, a hatchet clutched in his right hand.

If Hawk was not mistaken, this was the Comanche his companions facetiously called Comes Late.

He was well-named. Comes Late had indeed come late. Of the others in his war party, he alone, it seemed, was about to succeed where they had failed.

In Comanche, Comes Late said, "Before, you saw me run like a scared rabbit. I don't run anymore, Golden Hawk."

"I see that."

"Get up. You have a knife. We meet now in a fair fight."

"I do not want to kill you, Comes Late."

The Comanche smiled thinly. "Do not worry. You will not kill me. It is I who will kill you, Golden Hawk."

Drawing his knife, Hawk jumped to his feet and flung himself at the Comanche, knocking the rifle from his grasp. Hawk's first slash ripped open the Comanche, but Comes Late stood his ground and swung his hatchet with terrible force, its blade digging deeply into Hawk's side. The shock of it staggered Hawk, but he kept on his feet, put his head down, and rammed the Comanche backward.

The Indian lost his balance and tumbled into the pool. Hawk dived in after him, grabbed his head with both hands, and pushed him under the surface. Comes Late struggled desperately, his hatchet striking out blindly. Hawk leaned still more heavily upon the warrior's head, their blood darkening the water.

The hatchet dropped from the Indian's fingers. Comes Late's struggles grew less violent. Hawk was patient, and in a few seconds more, the Indian's thrashing had become feeble. Hawk kept the Comanche's head under a full minute longer, then released the Indian, watched his lifeless body float away, then staggered back out of the pool.

Glancing down at his wound, he decided woozily that he had better make for Fort Hall. Though he knew he was not thinking clearly, he pulled himself onto his horse and started off. Sometime during the next hour, he lost all sense of direction. Not long after, he was pitched from his horse. The cool grass cradled him gently. He felt himself slipping off into the darkness.

His horse pulled up a few yards farther on, gazed back at him curiously, then proceeded to crop the grass at its feet.

Someone was shaking him, hard. His teeth began to rattle. Opening his eyes, he saw Dick Wootton bent over him. The moment he saw Hawk open his eyes, Dick let Hawk go and sat back in the grass.

"You had me worried there for a minute, Hawk. How do you feel?"

"Weak—weak as a kitten."

"I checked. You got another hole in you. But it

ain't bleeding anymore. You had sense enough to fall on a bunch of pine needles. That stopped the bleeding, looks like. But I sure don't want to be around when they peel them off you."

"Help me onto my horse."

"Where are you heading?"

"Fort Hall."

"That sounds like a damn good idea."

As Dick helped Hawk over to his horse, Hawk asked, "What in hell're you doing this far west?"

"Heard you had trouble, Hawk. So I came looking for you."

"What about that new woman of yours?"

"She said she'd not be proud of me if I didn't go after you."

Hawk dragged his leg over the cantle. Once settled in the saddle, he looked down at Dick Wootton.

"Thanks, Dick. I mean for coming this far on my account. And I'd like to thank that new wife of your, too—if I make it as far as the fort."

"You'll make it, Hawk. Just hang on."

The pine needles that had scabbed the gash in Hawk's side dropped off before nightfall. Dick bandaged it tightly, but the bleeding continued, and for the next three days and nights, Hawk's temperature climbed, and with it his ability to separate nightmare from reality. Twice he ran off wildly; and on one of those occasions, when Dick tried to lead him back to their camp, Hawk went for him with his bowie.

By the time they reached Fort Hall, Hawk was close to death. But after a few days, he was out of danger. A week later he was on the mend, able to sit up in a chair outside the fort, drinking in the late summer's sun, and for the first time thinking of rebuilding his cabin. He would position it closer to the ridge this time so he'd get a better view of the valley and the mountains beyond.

Hawk gazed with a sick heart at the black ruin of what had once been his cabin. Only the fireplace and chimney remained standing. The walls were little more than piles of gray ash and charred logs. Where the floorboards had not been burned clear through, they had been ripped up and the ground under them filled with holes dug by the captain's men. More holes had been dug all around the cabin, mute testimony to the senseless lust for gold that had driven Smollett and his crew.

Hawk left the charred remains of his cabin and walked across the clearing to the site he was thinking of for another cabin. The view was spectacular. From this ridge he could see clear into the smoky valley far below, and to the snow-capped mountains beyond. He found, however, that the glimpse he had just had of his ruined cabin had punctured his enthusiasm. Furthermore, the chill in the air contained more than a hint of autumn. At this altitude the first snows would soon be upon him. Perhaps he was a fool to rebuild up here.

A familiar voice shouted his name. Glancing down the slope, he saw a rider emerging from the timber. It was Turnbolt!

Hawk waved and Turnbolt waved back. A moment later the two men were embracing warmly.

"You didn't get chewed up by Smollett's men," Hawk told him, pleased. "How in the hell did you manage that?"

"It wasn't my doing," Turnbolt replied grimly.

"What happened?"

"The deacon and Beechwood knew I was the one freed you. They came for me, blood in their eyes. I knocked the deacon over a pair of traces and lit out. It was a long walk before I reached Fort Hall. That's when I heard about you."

"I heard gunfire."

Turnbolt nodded bleakly. "It was pretty bad. Like you said, it wasn't only you the captain's men were after. Dick Wootton's leading a small army of mountain men after the bastards. I'm due to join up with them tomorrow. Right now I'm on a detour. I had something I wanted to give you."

Lifting Hawk's rifle out of his sling, Turnbolt handed it to him. Hawk took it from him almost reverently.

"Thanks, Don," was all he could manage.

"I knew how much store you put by it. And this here Colt's yours, too," he said, handing the revolver to Hawk.

"No. You keep the Colt, Don."

Pleased, Turnbolt took the sidearm back. "That was a long walk to Fort Hall, and this here revolver did come in mighty handy."

"Stay awhile," Hawk told him.

"Can't do that. I want to be with Wootton when he catches up with those butchers. Besides, three's a crowd."

"What in hell do you mean by that?"

Turnbolt swung back into his saddle. "You'll find out."

With a wave he turned his horse and rode back down the slope and vanished into the timber.

Examining the Hawken with a deep, humbling gratitude for its return, Hawk turned and walked back up the slope, then crossed the clearing to his mount and pack horse. As he slipped the Hawken into his saddle sling, he heard the soft pound of hooves crossing the clearing behind him. He turned.

And realized what Turnbolt had meant.

Raven Eyes was riding toward him.

She sat her paint with an easy grace that was breathtaking. Her face glowed with health. Behind her she trailed a pack horse pulling a travois, on which Hawk glimpsed buffalo hides and lodgepoles, along with piles of furs and a trunk full of household goods.

He walked, then ran to meet her as she flung herself from her pony, coming together with an impact that almost knocked them off their feet. Laughing, she clung to him.

With Raven Eyes' warm cheek against his, her arms tight about him, all thought of fleeing this mountain left Hawk. Soon Raven Eyes and he would be inside a warm tepee, a fire leaping in the hearth beside their bed of fresh pine boughs. Come snow, wind, or grizzly bear, he would proceed with the building of his new cabin.

And the next time he found gold he'd bury it, returning it to the ground from which it had been ripped. He had enough wealth in Raven Eyes and this beautiful, wild land.

SIGNET (0451)

BOLD NEW FRONTIERS

☐ **TEXAS ANTHEM by James Reno.** Johnny Anthem was a man of bold dreams—in a sprawling savage land as big and boundless as America in the making. There he discovered his "Yellow Rose of Texas" in the shining eyes of beautiful Rose McCain. Together they journeyed the blood-soaked trails of the brutal Texas wilderness burning with a dream they would fight for—live for—die for . . . staking their claims in the golden heart of the American dream. (143779—$3.50)

☐ **TEXAS BORN TEXAS ANTHEM II By James Reno.** A soaring American saga of courage and adventure. Johnny Anthem and his beautiful wife carved out a huge Texas ranch as a legacy for their twin sons. Their dreams are shattered when a son is abducted by a Mexican bandit and a daring rescue must be staged. Johnny was ready to defy every danger of nature and man to save his son and forge his family's destiny in a piece of America . . . For driving Johnny was a courage and strength that made him—and his country—great. (145607—$3.50)

☐ **THE BRANNOCKS by Matt Braun.** They are three brothers and their women—in a passionate, action-filled saga that sweeps over the vastness of the American West and shines with the spirit of the men and women who had the daring and heart to risk all to conquer a wild frontier land. (143442—$3.50)

☐ **WINDWARD WEST: The Brannocks #2 by Matt Braun.** Divided dreams pit brother against brother . . . each going his own way . . . until their paths cross and their conflicts exploded. This is their saga as they followed their dreams through the American western frontier where only the strongest survived. (147014—$3.50)

Prices slightly higher in Canada

Buy them at your local bookstore or use this convenient coupon for ordering.

NEW AMERICAN LIBRABY,
P.O. Box 999, Bergenfield, New Jersey 07621

Please send me the books I have checked above. I am enclosing $________
(please add $1.00 to this order to cover postage and handling). Send check or money order—no cash or C.O.D.'s. Prices and numbers subject to change without notice.

Name ________________________________

Address ________________________________

City________________State________________Zip Code________

Allow 4-6 weeks for delivery.
This offer is subject to withdrawal without notice.

SIGNET WESTERN (0451)

T.G. HORNE—A SENSATIONAL NEW WESTERN SERIES BY PIERCE MACKENZIE

☐ **T.G. HORNE #1: THE STOLEN WHITE EAGLE.** T.G. Horne bet his life on the turn of a card of the draw of a gun as he roamed the West in search of high-stake gaming and no-limit loving. Now he was aboard the stolen *White Eagle*, playing showdown with Enoch Hardaway, a poker wizard who'd never been beat. . . . (147111—$2.50)

☐ **T.G. HORNE #2: THE FLEECING OF FODDER CITY.** With an ace up his sleeve and a gun in his hand, T.G. Horne headed for Fodder City where the action looked like a sure bet to him. The town was ripe with gold and women ripe for loving and Horne soon found himself down to his last chip and bullet in a game where ladies were wild and killers held all the cards. . . . (157138—$2.75)

☐ **T.G. HORNE #3: WINNER TAKE NOTHING.** T.G. Horne was tops at playing stud and never met a man he couldn't outdraw in either a poker game or a shootout, or a lady he couldn't impress with his hard loving. But now he was searching for a swindler who had played him for a sucker. And in a game of no chance he had all the dice and guns loaded against him. . . . (147847—$2.50)

☐ **T.G. HORNE #4: THE SPANISH MONTE FIASCO.** Horne thought that beating a bunch of Mexicans at their own game would be easy. But the cards were marked against him when he got caught in a trap with a Mexican spitfire. Her double-crossing father had *Horne* marked—and he had to stop drawing aces and start drawing guns. (148630—$2.50)

Buy them at your local bookstore or use coupon on next page for ordering.

SIGNET BOOKS

BLAZING NEW TRAILS

(0451)

☐ **SHERRF JORY by Milton Bass.** With the town full of kill-crazy outlaws, Jory had not time to uncock his guns. Could Jory single-handedly stop this gang of blood thirsty killers? Nobody figured Jory had a chance against them ... until his bullets started flying and their bodies started falling. (148177—$2.75)

☐ **MISTR JORY by Milton Bass.** Jory's guns could spit fire ... but even he had his work cut out for him when he took on a big herd of cattle and a gunman faster on the draw than he could ever hope to be. (149653—$2.75)

☐ **DREAM WEST by David Nevin.** A fiery young officer and a sixteen-year-old politician's daughter—together they set out to defy every danger of nature and man to lead America across the Rockies to the Pacific ... to carve out a kingdom of gold ... and to create an epic saga of courage and love as great and enthralling as has ever been told ... (145380—$4.50)

☐ **ALL THE RIVERS RUN by Nancy Cato.** Here is the spellbinding story of a beautiful and vital woman—the men she loved, the children she bore, the dreams she followed, and the destiny she found in the lush, wild countryside and winding rivers of Victorian Australia. (125355—$3.95)

Prices slightly higher in Canada

Buy them at your local bookstore or use this convenient coupon for ordering.

NEW AMERICAN LIBRABY,
P.O. Box 999, Bergenfield, New Jersey 07621

Please send me the books I have checked above. I am enclosing $________ (please add $1.00 to this order to cover postage and handling). Send check or money order—no cash or C.O.D.'s. Prices and numbers subject to change without notice.

Name ____

Address ______________________________________

City______________State____________Zip Code________

Allow 4-6 weeks for delivery.
This offer is subject to withdrawal without notice.